PENGUIN BOOKS

How I Became Stupid

MARTIN PAGE was born in February 1975 and lives in Belleville, Paris. *How I Became Stupid* is his first novel and has been translated into twenty-four languages. The book had succeeded in not winning any literary prizes until recently, when it was given the Euregio-Schüler-Literaturpreis, awarded by Dutch and German high school students.

ADRIANA HUNTER is the English translator of eighteen books, including works by Geneviève Jurgensen, Agnès Desarthe, Amélie Nothomb, Frédéric Beigbeder, and Catherine Millet. She has been short-listed for the Independent Foreign Fiction Prize for the past three years (2001, 2002, 2003). She lives in Norfolk, England, with her husband and their three children.

how i
became
stupid

how i became stupid

Martin Page

translated by Adriana Hunter

 Penguin Books

PENGUIN BOOKS
Published by the Penguin Group
Penguin Group (USA) Inc., 375 Hudson Street, New York, New York 10014, U.S.A.
Penguin Group (Canada), 90 Eglinton Avenue East, Suite 700, Toronto, Ontario,
    Canada M4P 2Y3 (a division of Pearson Penguin Canada Inc.)
Penguin Books Ltd, 80 Strand, London WC2R 0RL, England
Penguin Ireland, 25 St Stephen's Green, Dublin 2, Ireland
    (a division of Penguin Books Ltd)
Penguin Group (Australia), 250 Camberwell Road, Camberwell, Victoria 3124,
    Australia (a division of Pearson Australia Group Pty Ltd)
Penguin Books India Pvt Ltd, 11 Community Centre, Panchsheel Park,
    New Delhi – 110 017, India
Penguin Group (NZ), 67 Apollo Drive, Rosedale, North Shore 0632, New Zealand
    (a division of Pearson New Zealand Ltd)
Penguin Books (South Africa) (Pty) Ltd, 24 Sturdee Avenue,
    Rosebank, Johannesburg 2196, South Africa

Penguin Books Ltd, Registered Offices: 80 Strand, London WC2R 0RL, England

First published in Penguin Books 2004

10

Translation copyright © Penguin Group (USA) Inc., 2004
All rights reserved

Originally published in French as *Comment je suis devenu stupide* by Le Dilettante,
Paris. © Le Dilettante, 2001.

LIBRARY OF CONGRESS CATALOGING-IN-PUBLICATION DATA
Page, Martin, 1975–
    [Comment je suis devenu stupide. English]
    How I became stupid / by Martin Page ; translated by
Adriana Hunter.
        p. cm.
    ISBN 978-0-14-200495-1
        I. Hunter, Adriana.   II. Title.
    PQ2716.A35C6613 2004
    843'.92—dc22   2004044644

Printed in the United States of America
Set in Old Style 7 with Journal Text • Designed by Sabrina Bowers

"He envied them all that they did not know."
—OSCAR WILDE,
"Lord Arthur Savile's Crime"

"Obladi oblada life goes on bra."
—THE BEATLES, "Ob-La-Di, Ob-La-Da,"
The White Album

how i
became
stupid

Antoine had always felt

he was living in dog years. When he was seven he felt about as playful as a man of forty-nine; by eleven he was as disillusioned as an old man of seventy-seven. Now, age twenty-five, Antoine was hoping to start taking it easy, and he resolved to shroud his brain in stupidity. He had already realized that intelligence was just the word people used for stupid remarks that were well presented and prettily pronounced, and that intelligence itself was so corrupt, there was often more to be gained from being dumb than from being a sworn intellectual. Intelligence makes you unhappy, lonely, and poor, whereas disguising it offers the possibility of immortality in newsprint and the admiration of those who believe what they read.

The kettle started whistling feebly. Antoine poured the simmering water into a blue cup with a motif of a moon between two red roses. The tea leaves unfurled as they spun round, diffusing their color and flavor while the steam vanished and mingled with the air. Antoine sat down at his desk, facing the only window in his untidy little studio.

He had spent the night writing. After quite a few

false starts and pages of rough notes in his college-
ruled notebook, he had finally managed to give his
manifesto some sort of coherent form. He had spent
the last few weeks in an exhaustive search for an
escape, attempting to formulate some evasive action,
but had eventually confronted the terrifying truth
that his own mind was the cause of his unhappiness,
and there was no escaping that. On that July night,
then, Antoine began writing down the arguments
which explained his decision to renounce all intelligent thought. This notebook would bear witness
to his plan (in the event that he did not emerge
unscathed from this perilous experiment). And also
perhaps serve to remind himself when the burden
grew too great to bear that this ridiculous undertaking was once justified by lucid scientific thought.

A robin tapped on the window with its beak.
Antoine looked up from his book and tapped back
with his pen. He took a sip of tea, stretched in his
chair, and, running a hand through his slightly greasy
hair, thought he really did have to steal more shampoo from the Champion grocery store on the corner.
Antoine didn't feel like a thief. He wasn't nimble
enough for it, so he took only what he needed: a blob
of shampoo squeezed discreetly into a little candy
box. He proceeded in the same way with toothpaste,
soap, shaving cream, grapes, and cherries; extracting
just his tithe, he foraged and nibbled his way round

department stores and supermarkets every day. Similarly (as he didn't have enough money to buy all the books he wanted, and having noted the acuity of the security officers and the sensitivity of the antitheft barriers in the FNAC music superstore), he stole books one page at a time and then reconstructed them in the safety of his apartment like a clandestine editor. Each page won by criminal means took on a far greater symbolic importance than if it had been neatly stuck between its siblings; taken out of the book, spirited away, and then patiently bound back with the others, it became sacred. Antoine's bookcase contained some twenty books reconstituted in this way—his precious and individual limited editions.

By the time the sun was beginning to rise, exhausted by his sleepless night, he was about ready to write a conclusion to his proclamation. After hesitating for a moment with the end of his pen in his mouth, he started to write, his head tilted close to the book and his tongue peeping out between his lips:

Nothing annoys me more than those stories where, at the end, the hero is in the same situation as the beginning but he's gained something. He's taken risks, survived adventures but, in the end, lands back on his feet. I don't want to be a part of that lie: pretending I don't already know how all this will end. I know full well that this journey into stupidity is going to turn into a hymn to intelligence. It will be my own personal little Odyssey—after my share of trials and dangerous adventures I will end up back in Ithaca. I can already smell the ouzo and the stuffed grape leaves. It would be hypocritical not to admit it, not to say that, right from the beginning, you know the hero's going to come out okay, he's even going to come out of it a better man. The conclusion—painfully contrived to seem natural—will proclaim a moral along these lines: "It is good to think, but we must make the most of this life." Whatever we say and whatever we do, there is always a moral grazing somewhere in the meadows of our personalities.

It is Wednesday, July 19. The sun has at last decided to come out of retirement. At the end of this adventure I'd like to be able to say, like the character Joker in Full Metal Jacket: *"I'm in a world of shit . . . yes. But I am alive. And I am not afraid."*

Antoine put down his pen and closed his book. He took a sip of tea; but it had gone cold. He stretched and started boiling more water on the little gas camping stove that stood directly on the floorboards. The robin tapped on the window with its beak. Antoine opened the window and put a handful of sunflower seeds on the sill.

Half of Antoine's family were originally from Burma. His paternal grandparents had come to France in the 1930s to follow in the footsteps of Shan, their illustrious ancestor who had discovered Europe eight centuries earlier. Shan—a woman—was a botanist adventurer; she was interested in the arts and in remedies, and was trying to draw up a map of the region. After each expedition she went back to Pagan, her birthplace, to be with her family and to share her discoveries with them and with the men of letters. Anawratha, the first great Burmese sovereign, caught wind of her passion for research and adventure, and gave her the material and financial means to discover the vast unknown world. For months on end Shan and her crew traveled by land and sea, and lost themselves sufficiently enough to find their way to the New World, Europe. By crossing the Mediterranean they landed in the south of France and soon reached Paris. They offered glass beads and cheap silk to the natives of the Europeans lands, and made trading agreements with the chiefs of these pale-faced tribes. Shan returned to her own country to a triumphant reception thanks to her discovery; she became a celebrated figure and ended her days in glory. Amid the upheavals and violence of the twentieth century, Antoine's grandparents decided to follow in their forebear's footsteps in the hopes of finding comparable happiness. They had, therefore, settled in Brittany in the early thirties; in 1941 they even set up the famous Resistance network FTP Burma. They had gradually integrated themselves, had learned to speak Breton and, with rather more difficulty, to like oysters.

Antoine's mother was a coastal inspector for the Department of the Environment, and she was Breton by birth; his father was Burmese and he divided his time between his passion for cooking and his activities as a fisherman on a trawler. When Antoine was eighteen, he had left his attentive and anxious parents to head for the capital, hoping to make his own way in life. As a child his ambition had been to become Bugs Bunny; then later, when he was more mature, he had wanted to be Vasco da Gama. But his career adviser had said he would have to study something that was featured on the documentation from the Ministry of Education. His university career followed the same labyrinthine route as his passions, as he was always finding he had new ones. Antoine had never understood the arbitrary way in which subjects were delineated: he went to the classes that interested him in whatever

discipline they might be, and skipped those for which
the lecturers were not up to the job. It was, therefore,
more or less by chance that he validated his diplomas
thanks to an accumulation of diverse courses and
modules.

He had few friends, because he suffered from that
sort of social awkwardness which comes from too
much tolerance and understanding. His liking for so
many such disparate things automatically banished
him from groups formed on the basis of dislikes.
True, he didn't like crowds much, but it was actually
his curiosity and passion—both perfectly innocent of
boundaries and clans—that made him feel like a
lonely foreigner in his own country. In a world where
public opinion is reduced to *yes, no,* and *not sure,*
Antoine couldn't tick any of the boxes. For him, being *for* or *against* was an unbearable limitation on a
complex question. On top of this, he was endowed
with a gentle shyness that he clung to like some
vestige of childhood. It seemed to him that a human
being was so vast and so rich a thing that it was im-
possibly vain to be overconfident with others, with
strangers and with all the uncertainties that each
individual represented. At one point he was afraid
he might lose his little shy streak and join the great
mass of people who despise you if you don't dominate
them; but, by a grittily determined act of will, he
managed to save it like an oasis of his personality. He

may have been hurt, frequently and deeply, but this had in no way hardened his character; he kept intact his extreme sensitivity, which, like a phoenix, rose back up purer than ever each time it was damaged and bruised. In short, even if he did have moderate faith in himself, he tried not to believe himself too readily, not to acquiesce too easily to what he was thinking, because he knew his own mind was not above deceiving him to comfort himself.

Before reaching the decision that he had to change his existence so dramatically (before, that is, becoming stupid), Antoine tried a number of other options, other attempts to resolve the fact that he found it difficult to participate in this life.

Trying to become an alcoholic was his first attempt (which might be deemed misguided but which he undertook with the sincerest of hopes).

———

Antoine had never touched a drop of alcohol. Even when he injured himself slightly, when he grazed himself, good abstainer that he was, he would refuse to disinfect the wound with 60-proof alcohol, preferring to use antiseptic creams.

At home there had been no wine and no aperitifs. Later, he had been contemptuous of using fermented or distilled concoctions to compensate for a lack of imagination or to dispel the effects of depression.

Having noticed that when people are drunk their ideas are vague and quite unrelated to any notion of reality, that their sentences seem perfectly satisfied with incoherence, and, to cap it all, that they themselves seem to think they are uttering profound truths, Antoine decided to adhere to this promising philosophy. Drunkenness seemed a good way to suppress any tendency his intellect might have to reflect on life. If he were drunk, he would no longer need to think, he would no longer be able to: his rhetoric would consist of lyrical, eloquent, and voluble approximations. Cushioned in so much drunkenness, intelligence would no longer have any meaning; having broken from his moorings, he might be shipwrecked or eaten by sharks without even worrying about it. Laughing for no reason, making absurd exclamations, in a state of inebriation he would love everyone and lose his inhibitions. How he would dance and twirl! But, of course, he would not lose sight of the darker side of alcohol: the hangovers, the nausea, looming cirrhosis. And the addiction.

He had every intention of becoming an alcoholic. It keeps you busy. Alcohol occupies every thought and provides a goal in times of despair: getting better. Then he would go to Alcoholics Anonymous meetings, would tell his story, would be supported and understood by creatures like himself applauding his courage and his will to break free. He would be an alcoholic—in other words, someone with an illness that is recognized by society. Alcoholics are pitied, they are cared for, they are thought of in medical terms, humanely. But no one thinks of pitying intelligent people: "He watches human behavior, that must make him very unhappy"; "My niece is very intelligent, but she's a really nice girl. She's hoping to grow out of it"; "For a while there, I was afraid you might become intelligent." Those are the sort of well-meaning and compassionate words he should have been entitled to if there were any justice in the world. But no, intelligence is a double curse: it makes you suffer, and no one thinks of it as an illness.

Being an alcoholic would be a social promotion by comparison. He would suffer from visible afflictions, with a known cause and existing treatments; there are no detoxing cleanses for intelligence. Just as thinking produces a certain exclusion—in the distance between the observer and the observed—being an alcoholic would be a way of finding a place. And being perfectly integrated in society, if they haven't achieved it naturally, must be the dream of every alcoholic. Thanks to the alcohol, they no longer have any reserve in the game of human life and can slip into it quite happily.

Having absolutely no knowledge of the subject,

Antoine didn't know how to launch into his new
career. Should he start by going on a succession of
benders or, quite the opposite, take slow, careful
steps into the swamplands of alcohol?

He couldn't help it: his enduring curiosity
persuaded him to rush to the municipal library in
Montreuil, a stone's throw from his apartment. He
wanted to become an alcoholic intelligently, in a
constructive, cultured way, to know the secrets of
this poison that was to save him. Antoine ferreted
through the shelves, selected the books that struck
him as the most interesting under the condescending
eye of the librarian (himself deeply convinced of his
intelligence because he was badly dressed). He knew
Antoine well; this was the fourth consecutive year
that he had been named "Reader of the Year."
Despite Antoine's protestations in the face of this
cultural exhibitionism, the librarian had displayed a
photocopy of his library card with an inscription in
bold print: "Reader of the Year." Ridiculous!

Antoine arrived at the counter with his *Dictionary of Alcohol Across the World, A Historical Guide
to Spirits, Spirits and Wines, The World's Greatest
Alcoholic Drinks, A Compendium of Alcohol.*

The librarian registered the loans and exclaimed,
"Still more! You're going to break your last year's
record, congratulations. Are you doing some historical research on alcohol?"

"No, actually, I'm . . . I'm trying to become an alcoholic. But before starting to drink I felt I wanted to know my subject."

The librarian spent the next few days wondering whether that had been a joke; then he died, mysteriously suffocated under a group of German tourists near the Eiffel Tower.

———

After spending three days devouring the books, making notes and marking up key passages, Antoine felt he had a good grip on the subject, and he searched through his address book for an acquaintance who might be able to teach him his methods. Someone who had it in him to be a professor of wines and spirits, a Plato of liquor, an Einstein of brandy, a Newton of vodka . . . the Yoda of whiskey. Combing through friends, immediate family, distant relations, colleagues, and neighbors, he came upon psychotics, Catholics, a baron, a crossword fanatic, a farting expert, a heroine addict, supporters of various political parties . . . and plenty of other damaged individuals. But not one alcoholic.

Just along the sidewalk from his apartment there was a bistro called Captain Elephant. This was where he decided to do his prospecting.

Antoine took his books as well as a little writing
pad to make a note of all his forthcoming experiences
and all the new acquaintances he hoped to make.
As he opened the door it rang a little bell, but no
one turned round to see who had come in. He looked
at the customers, trying to gauge who might qualify
to be his instructor. It was only eight-thirty in the
morning, but they were drinking heartily already.
There were only men, some of them young but most
of them over forty; they had that slight patina, that
quality typical of alcoholics that made it difficult to
determine their age. Their damaged lives had failed
to give them a taste for more healthy passions, and
so they spent what little they had on the substitutes
for happiness and beauty provided by alcohol.

The bar was like a thousand others: zinc counter,
bottles lined up like the soldiers in a secret army, an
old jukebox . . . and, most characteristically, that
cocktail of smells, of cigarettes, coffee, alcohol, and
cleaning products, which pervaded every memory.

There was a man wearing a scruffy old cap sitting at the bar, and he had lined up eleven glasses
filled with different-colored liquids. Antoine deduced
that he was a specialist. Still unsure of himself, he
put his books down on the bar. The man didn't so
much as look his way before emptying the first glass.
By casting his mind back to the photographs in his

encyclopedia, Antoine identified the various drinks and named them, pointing to each one in turn: "Port, gin, red wine, Calvados, whiskey, brandy, lager, Guinness, Bloody Mary, and that one's probably champagne. The red wine might be a Bordeaux, and you've just had a pastis."

The man in the cap looked at Antoine suspiciously. Then, seeing how inoffensive he looked—clean, young, mop of hair—he smiled.

"Not bad," he conceded. "You've got a gift, kid." And he knocked back the glass of whiskey.

"Thank you, sir."

"Is that your job, then, recognizing drinks? That's pretty original but I'm darned if I know what use you could put it to. There's usually a label on the bottle."

"No," said Antoine, shaking his head and discreetly turning away from the man's well-loaded breath. "I'm reading about alcohol to find out how it's made, what ingredients are used. . . . I want to know everything about it."

"What use is that going to be to you?" the man said with a smile, having just emptied the glass of gin.

"I want to become an alcoholic."

The man closed his eyes and clenched the glass in his hand; his knuckles went white, the glass made a creaking sound. There were noises coming in from the street, passing cars and lively conversations among shopkeepers. The man took in a deep breath and blew it out gently. He opened his eyes again and held his hand out to Antoine. He was smiling again.

"My name is Léonard."

"Pleased to meet you. Um, I'm Antoine."

They shook hands. Léonard watched Antoine, intrigued and amused. They were still shaking hands. Antoine eventually disengaged himself.

"You want to become an alcoholic. . . . ," mumbled Léonard. "Twenty years ago I would have thought you were a hallucination, but it's been a while now that the drink only ever serves me up reality in these mirages. You want to become an alcoholic, and that's why you've got all these books. That figures."

"These books are for . . . I don't want to become an alcoholic any old way. I'm really interested in it, in all the different kinds of alcohol, spirits, liqueurs, wines; there's so much variety! I've found out that alcohol is connected to the history of mankind, and can boast more followers than Christianity, Buddhism, and Islam put together. At the moment I'm reading a fascinating essay by Raymond Dumay on the subject. . . ."

"If you read too much you'll never become an alcoholic," Léonard commented phlegmatically.

"We're talking about something that takes quite some commitment. You have to give up several hours a day to it. You could say it's an Olympic discipline. I don't know if you've got it in you, kid."

"Look, I don't want to brag, but . . . well, I speak Aramaic, I've learned how to repair First World War fighter planes, to produce honey, to change the diapers on my neighbor's dog, and when I was fifteen I spent a month's holiday with my uncle Joseph and my aunt Miranda. So, with your help, I think I'm quite capable of becoming an alcoholic. I've got the determination."

"With my help?" Léonard asked with kindly surprise. He looked into his glass of champagne—with its little bubbles rising up to the surface—and laughed.

"Yes. I know the theory, but I haven't had any practice. But you," said Antoine, pointing at the row of glasses, "you strike me as an expert."

Léonard sucked the glassful of cognac into his mouth and held it there for a moment. The bartender wiped the counter with his cloth and cleared away the empty glasses. Léonard frowned.

"And who's told you you've got any aptitude for it? Do you really think you can become an alcoholic just like that? That you just have to want to and to have a few drinks? I know people who've spent their whole lives drinking, but who've never managed to become alcoholics. They weren't cut out for it. So you . . . you think you've got the gift? You pitch up here saying you want to become an alcoholic as if the world owed it to you! Let me tell you something, young man: it's the drink that chooses; it's the drink that decides if you've got it in you to be a wino."

Antoine shrugged his shoulders, crestfallen: he had never been so presumptuous as to think it would be easy, which was precisely why he had come to look for a coach in this bistro. Léonard had reacted with all the indignation of an old sailor hearing a naïve and inexperienced youngster say he wants to go to sea. Having spent his childhood idling round little ports in Brittany, it was a response that Antoine recognized, and one he understood: craftsmen are proud and proprietary of their art.

"I didn't mean to give that impression, Mr. Léonard. I confess my ignorance, and I've no idea whether I have any gift for it. I'm asking you to take me on as a pupil. You could teach me."

"I don't mind trying, kid," Léonard replied, flattered, "but I can't give you any guarantees. If you don't have what it takes . . . Not everyone can become an alcoholic, that's for sure, there's a process of selection; it's a sad fact, but that's life. So don't blame me if you get left on the shore. There are other boats to catch."

"I understand."

Léonard hesitated between the Bloody Mary and
the glass of Guinness. He opted for the stout. Some
of the froth settled in the gray hairs of his beard, and
he wiped them off on the thick navy blue cloth of the
back of his sleeve.

"Good. I need to ask you a few questions. A sort
of preliminary test."

"Like an entrance exam?"

"Come on, kid, you've gotta understand that
there are conditions when it comes to being an alcoholic, it's a serious business. . . ."

"But you don't actually need a license," said
Antoine with a shrug and smile.

"You should, though. Some people just can't
handle their liquor; they beat their wives and children, drive like lunatics, and they have the vote. . . .
The state should take responsibility for training alcoholics, so that they know their limits, and realize
there are changes in their understanding of time and
space, and in their personalities. . . . Like with swim-
ming, it's better to make sure you can swim before
jumping into the pool."

"In this particular instance," Antoine ventured,
"you're more likely to be checking that I'll be able to
sink."

"Absolutely right, kid. I want to know if you've
got the fins to sink. Let's see . . . First question: why

do you want to become an alcoholic? I'd say it's fundamental, understanding the motive."

Antoine rubbed his forehead as he thought about it. He looked at the other customers in the bistro and noticed how perfectly they fit the decor. It was almost as if they were related to one another—not because they looked alike, but because they appeared to all be made of the same sorry stuff.

"The cause of alcoholism is 'ugliness and the complete baffling sterility of existence as it is *sold* to you.'"

"Is that a quote?" asked Léonard after downing the Bloody Mary in one gulp.

"Yes, from Malcolm Lowry."

"One question, kid: when you go to buy bread do you quote Shakespeare to the baker? 'To buy all-butter croissants or burger buns, that is the question.' I'd prefer it if you did the talking instead of calling on some goddamned writer. If you want my opinion, it's too easy, quoting other people, because there are so many great writers who've said so many great things that no one would ever need to express their own opinions ever again."

"Well, let's say that I'm poor and I don't have any future. . . . But most of all I think too much, I can't help overanalyzing myself and the world around me, trying to understand how this whole crazy circus works. . . . It makes me incredibly sad to know that we're not free, and that even each conscious thought or act is made at the cost of a wound that will never heal."

"Kid, what you're saying is you're depressed. . . ."

"That's my natural state. I've been suffering from depression for twenty-five years."

Léonard gave Antoine a friendly pat on the back. A customer came in and sat down at a table where a group of men were playing cards. He ordered a cup of coffee and a glass of Calvados. The bartender switched on the radio to listen to the nine o'clock news bulletin.

"But alcohol's not going to cure you, you know. You mustn't believe that. It'll soothe your wounds, but it'll give you others, and they may be worse. You won't be able to get by without drink, and even if, in the early days, you get feelings of euphoria, if the drinking makes you happy, that soon goes and all that's left is the tyranny of dependence and need. Your life'll be reduced to mist, semiconsciousness, hallucinations, paranoia, tremors, fits of delirium, bouts of violence toward anyone around you. Your personality will fall apart. . . ."

"That's what I want!" Antoine said emphatically, drumming his little fist on the bar. "I don't have the strength to be me anymore. I've lost the heart or the will to have anything like a personality. My personality is a luxury that's costing me too dearly. I just want to be a bland presence. I've had enough of my freedom of thought, of everything I know and of my goddamned consciousness!"

Léonard emptied the glass of port, then pursed his lips. He stayed like that, thinking, with the glass in the air, looking at himself in the mirror, which was partly obscured by the bottles behind the bar. As he worked his way through the glasses, he was slumping more heavily on the bar, his eyes were narrowing, and, at the same time, his movements were becoming less shaky, more expansive and fluent. For his last question of the "examination," Léonard asked Antoine to guess why he had lined up eleven glasses of different drinks on the bar.

"So that none of them felt jealous?" Antoine replied straight away.

"So that none of them felt jealous. . . . ," Léonard whispered with a smile, gently knocking one of the glasses rhythmically on the bar. "Could you be more precise?"

"Maybe it's your way of showing your respect, in equal measure, to all these different kinds of alcohol. You're not a lover of beer or Scottish whiskey, nothing as sectarian as that: you like alcohol in all its forms. You're in love with Alcohol with a capital *A*."

"I'd never thought of it like that but . . . Yes, I agree. Antoine, Antoine . . . I think you've got what it takes. Mother Nature in her great mercy may have given you the gift. But I should really tell you about all the problems you're going to have. You'll do a lot of puking; your stomach will be tied in knots and full of acid; you'll have all sorts of migraines—in your eyes, in your head—aching in your neck, your muscles, and your bones; you'll have ulcers, problems with your eyesight, trouble sleeping, hot flashes, panic attacks, a lot of diarrhea. All in exchange for a little bit of warmth and comfort here and there. I just thought you should know."

Two more customers came in. They shook hands with the bartender and waved hello to Léonard. They sat at a table at the back of the bistro, lit their pipes, and drank beer while they shared a copy of *Le Monde*. Antoine looked at Léonard quite openly. As usual he was very calm and very sure of his decision. He ran his hand through his hair, mussing it up.

"It's what I want, I want a different kind of torment, real pains, physical manifestations of a particular type of behavior. And drink will be the cause of my problems; not the truth, but drink. I prefer an illness you can hold within the walls of a bottle to some intangible, omnipotent illness I can't put a name to. I'll know why I'm in pain. Alcohol will occupy my every thought, it'll fill every second of my life, like filling a succession of little glasses. . . ."

"I agree," said Léonard after stroking his beard for a moment. "I'd like to be your instructor in alcoholism. I'll be strict—I'm going to make you work. It's a long-term apprenticeship, almost a form of asceticism."

"Thank you, thank you from the bottom of my heart," Antoine said calmly, shaking the drunkard's coarse, dry hand.

Léonard raised one hand and snapped his fingers to call the bartender, who was reading *Le Parisien* at the far end of the bar, near the till.

"Roger, a draft beer for the kid!"

The bartender put the beer down in front of Antoine.

"Thank you. We're going to start gently. This beer is just five-percent alcohol, it'll slip down easily. You need to get your palate used to it, get your spring chicken of a liver acclimated. You don't become an alcoholic by going on a bender every Saturday evening; it takes perseverance and constant application. There's nothing methodical about the way most people become alcoholics. They drink whiskey or vodka in huge quantities, make themselves sick, and start drinking again. If you want my opinion, Antoine, they're assholes. Assholes and amateurs! It's perfectly easy to become an alcoholic much more intelligently, by carefully calibrating the quantity and the percentage of alcohol."

Antoine looked at the tall glass of beer crowned with white froth; and everything he saw through this prism looked golden. Léonard took off his cap and pulled it down over Antoine's head.

"Go on, my friend, you mustn't be frightened, you're not going to drown in there."

"Do I drink it all in one shot," asked Antoine, feeling somewhat intimidated, "or in little sips?"

"That's for you to find out. If you like the taste and if you don't want to get drunk too quickly, drink it in little sips, savor this nectar of hops. Otherwise, if you find it too disgusting, down the whole lot."

After sniffing at his beer and getting some froth on his nose, Antoine started to drink. He winced and pursed his face, and had another sip.

Within five minutes an ambulance screeched around the corner and skidded to a halt on the sidewalk outside Captain Elephant. Two paramedics armed with a stretcher burst into the bar and carried off Antoine, who was in the depths of an alcoholic coma. Sitting on the bar was his glass of beer. It was still half full.

Due to an extreme physiological sensitivity, Antoine was unable to become an alcoholic. As a substitute remedy he resolved to commit suicide. Being an alcoholic had been his final ambition in his bid for social integration; bringing about his own death was the ultimate means he could find to participate in this world. Various people he admired had had the courage to choose the time of their own deaths: Hemingway, Virginia Woolf (whom he adored), his beloved Seneca, Debord, Caton D'Utique, Sylvia Plath, Demosthenes, Cleopatra, Lafargue . . .

Life was nothing but endless torture. He no longer felt any pleasure watching the sun rise, his every waking moment was sour, ruining the taste of anything that could have brought him enjoyment. As he had never really felt that he was living, he was not afraid of death. He was even happy that, in death, he would find the sole proof that he had been alive. The unbelievably poor quality of the food he had been given since he had been in the hospital only contributed to his conviction that he should take his own life.

Antoine had been admitted to the accident and emergency department of the Pitié-Salpêtriere Hospital, in spite of the laminated card in his wallet which stated that he would donate his organs in the instance of brain death, and that he would rather die in agony on the sidewalk than be treated at La Pitié. The reason he would do anything rather than end up in that hospital was that he ran the risk of meeting his uncle Joseph and his aunt Miranda there. Antoine was kind-natured but he could not stand them; in fact, no one could stand them. It was not that they were dangerous, only that they never stopped complaining, moaning, and making a fuss about the least little thing. A group of delightful Buddhists had been reduced to joining the ranks of a paramilitary force as a result of spending too much time with them. Every time they traveled abroad they created a diplomatic incident. As a result they were forbidden to visit several countries: Israel, Switzerland, the Netherlands, Japan, and the United States. The IRA, ETA, and Hezbollah had published bulletins stating that they would execute the couple if they set foot in their territories again. The authorities in the relevant countries said and did nothing that implied any opposition to this stance. Perhaps one day the army would have the courage to use the destructive potential of this couple and would deploy it when atomic bombs were discovered to be too

ineffectual. For years now Uncle Joseph and Aunt
Miranda had been spending all their time in the hospital, changing departments and floors according to
their operations and illnesses, either genuine ones or
those invented by their feverish hypochondria. They
visited every department in turn, transferring from
urology to allergies, trying angiology, gastroenterol-
ogy, otorhinolaryngology, stomatology, dermatology,
diabetology . . . And so they traveled round the hos-
pitals in the capital as if they were exotic countries,
always avoiding the two departments that could
have done something to help them (and the rest of
the world): psychiatry and forensic medicine.

Antoine tried without success to persuade the
nurses to strike his name from the hospital register
to avoid a visit from his aunt and uncle. While
slowly recovering from his coma, he reached his
decision to commit suicide as he sat in his hospital
bed, a plastic spoon sticking out of his little cup of
lumpy, pink apple compote.

His friends—Ganja, Charlotte, Aaslee, and
Rodolphe—came to visit him. Ganja, a former co-
disciple at the Faculty of Biology, was the most laid-
back man in the world, the very embodiment of
goodwill. He had made something of a habit of com-
forting Antoine by using the most extraordinary
medicinal plants to prepare herbal infusions for him,
and these had certainly brightened their evenings

27

together. They played chess several times a week at
the top of the observatory at the Sorbonne, and they
would also wander through the streets of Paris
chatting. Antoine had no idea what Ganja's profession might be, for he remained very mysterious on
the subject, but he had a fair amount of money so
he was frequently the one who picked up the bills.
Charlotte worked as a translator for a publishing
company and had once been Antoine's neighbor.
Her great dream was to have a child but, being a
lesbian, she had no desire to achieve this by natural
means. Therefore, she regularly had herself artifi-
cially inseminated, thanks to a doctor friend. To improve her chances after each insemination, Antoine
would take her to the Foire du Trône (or any other
convenient fun fair) and go round on the big wheel
with her for hours at a time. It was not a very scientific technique, but Charlotte felt that the centrifugal
force of these contraptions would propel the recalci-
trant sperm to the right place. Rodolphe, a colleague
from the university, was the statutory contrarian.
He was two years older than Antoine and was responsible for running a philosophy class entitled
Kant and the Reign of Absolute Thought. Rodolphe
was a pure product of the education system and
could expect to be appointed as an assistant professor within the next two years, to be promoted to
university professor in about seven years, and to die

in perfect obscurity some sixty years later, leaving a body of work that would influence generations of termites. What they had in common, what brought Antoine and Rodolphe together, was the fact that they never agreed on anything. Their last argument had been about thought: Rodolphe, philosopher that he was, stated that he produced acts of pure thought simply by activating his all-powerful desire to exercise his perfectly free will. Antoine laughed at him, reminding him of all the contingencies and countless determining factors governing human beings. But Rodolphe did not seem to think that the same sun shone on a professor of philosophy as on ordinary mortals. To summarize, Antoine represented doubt, Rodolphe certainty, and you could say that they each exaggerated his leanings in his own way. Finally, Aaslee was Antoine's best friend, but we will talk more about him later.

When they first came to visit him in the hospital, Ganja brought an herbal infusion, Charlotte some flowers, Aaslee a five-foot-tall dwarf palm in a pot, and Rodolphe was sorry Antoine was not hooked up to an artificial ventilator that he could have unplugged.

His friends' concern did nothing to change Antoine's silent resolve: for once in his life he had decided to be selfish despite the pain and irritation it might cause his friends.

———

In the bed next to Antoine there was a human being, that much was clear, but Antoine could not have been more specific than that. He didn't know whether it was a man or a woman, and didn't even know what sort of age he or she might be for the simple reason that the patient was wrapped in bandages like an Egyptian mummy. It turned out that this white form was not sheltering the remains of some lost pharaoh because when it finally spoke, it had a woman's voice with no trace of an accent from the valley of the kings: "Don't you worry, I'll be all right. Once again . . . I'll be all right."

"I'm sorry?" asked Antoine, sitting up in bed.

"What are you here for?" said the voice.

"Alcoholic coma."

"Oh, I've already tried that," the woman said lightly. "It's not bad. What did you drink. Whiskey? Vodka?"

"Beer."

"How many liters?"

"Half a glass."

"Half a glass? As drinking goes, you've set something of a record, then! Yes, alcoholic coma's one of the classics."

"That wasn't what I was aiming for. I wanted to be an alcoholic, but it didn't work. I now think sui-

cide's the most manageable solution. At least with
that I've got a hell of a chance."

"Don't you be so sure: it's the most difficult
thing, doing away with yourself. It's easier to get
your high school diploma, become a police inspector,
or get your master's degree in literature than to
commit suicide. The success rate is less than eight
percent."

Antoine sat on the edge of his bed. The pale sun
filtered through the slats of the venetian blinds and
cast its feeble light on the drear-colored walls of the
ward. Antoine's friends had come by a few hours
earlier, but no one ever came to see the woman.

"Did you try to commit suicide?" Antoine asked.

"I'm such a failure." She looked away.

"Was it not your first attempt?"

"I don't count them any longer, it's too depress-
ing. I've tried everything, mind you. But each time
something or someone gets in the way. Of my
death, that is. When I tried to drown myself some
brave half-wit went and saved me. In fact he died a
few days later of pneumonia. Awful, isn't it? When I
hanged myself the rope broke. When I fired a bullet
into my temple, it went right through my head
without touching my brain or causing any serious
damage. I swallowed two bottles of sleeping pills,
but the lab had made a mistake with the dosage so I
just got a three-day nap. Three months ago I even

31

took on a hired killer to do me in, but the moron got it wrong and killed my neighbor! I really don't have any luck. At first I wanted to commit suicide because I was in despair, but now the main reason for my despair is that I can't seem to commit suicide."

The only part of her that could be seen through the white bandages were her green eyes; they looked like emeralds nestling in a white casket. Antoine tried to find a trace of sadness in them, but could see only annoyance.

"You want to know why I'm in this state?" she asked, turning to look at Antoine. "Don't be embarrassed, anyone would want to ask why I'm trussed up like this. I threw myself off the top story of the Eiffel Tower. It should have been foolproof, shouldn't it? Well, it just happened that at exactly that moment a group of German tourists huddled together for a souvenir photo."

"And you fell on the Germans?"

"Yes, I crushed them. They cushioned my fall. I even bounced. Several times. Net result: almost every bone in my body is broken but, according to that dolt of a doctor, I'll be back on my feet and raring to go in six months!"

Silence gradually spread its great, fragile butterfly wings across the ward. The sun had disappeared, replaced by gray and rain. This particular month of July was reading the script for March.

"Maybe you should stop trying to commit suicide—you just keep hurting other people. It's going
to end in massacre. Try . . . I don't know . . . meeting
people, listening to Clash albums, falling in love . . ."

"You don't understand!" she retorted sharply.
"It's all because of love that I want to kill myself, so
if I fall in love again and it goes wrong, I'm going to
want to be dead twice over. And anyway, suicide's
my vocation; I've been crazy about it ever since I
was a little girl. What's it going to look like if I die of
natural causes at age ninety?"

"I don't know, I just don't know."

"That's not going to happen; I won't suffer the
humiliation. I eat garbage, loads of fried food and
tons of meat, I drink too much, I smoke two packs a
day . . . do you think that's a viable route to suicide?"

"Yes," Antoine said encouragingly. "All are well-
intended means to an end. But, having said that, I
don't think you'll be recorded as a suicide in the
statistics if you die of lung cancer, even if that was
what you were trying for."

"Don't you worry, I'm not going to fail again."

The woman then told Antoine that on the notice
board at the town hall in the Eighteenth Arrondissement, among the yoga and pottery classes, she had
spotted a notice for a suicide course. Antoine, who
had no experience in this field and didn't want to
waste precious years of death in unsuccessful

attempts at killing himself, listened to his fellow patient with considerable attention. She told him her
plans: as soon as she had recovered she would go
along to the class and, with great application, learn
how to go about killing herself properly. She
dictated the telephone number for the class to
Antoine.

The door was suddenly flung open and two Tas-
manian devils appeared in a flurry of exclamations
and twirling hands: Uncle Joseph and Aunt Miranda
threw themselves at poor Antoine. They asked for
news of him and of his family but digressed to their
own interests—in other words, their ailments. Uncle
Joseph told Antoine and his fellow patient—who
must have been regretting the presence of the German tourists more than ever—that he had just had
an operation on his spleen and was convinced that
the surgeon had swapped his spleen for someone
else's. He insisted that Antoine touch his side: "Can
you feel the spleen, Antoine?" he muttered between
clenched teeth. "There, can you feel it? It's not my
spleen—they won't get away with this—it's not my
spleen!"

"Come on, Uncle Joseph, why would they have
swapped your spleen?"

"Why?" exclaimed his uncle. "Why? Tell him,
Miranda, I just can't. Tell him, Miranda!"

"Why?" Aunt Miranda picked up the conversation. "Organ trafficking!"

"Keep it down!" cried Uncle Joseph. "Keep it down, they'll hear you, and God knows what they'll do to us. They'll do anything, anything. People who swap spleens will do anything!"

"We think it's a conspiracy," whispered Aunt Miranda, taking Antoine's arm. "We've got together a whole body of evidence and speculation about a major organ-trafficking racket right here in this hospital."

"What makes you think that?" asked Antoine.

"The spleen!" exclaimed Uncle Joseph. "My spleen! Isn't that proof enough? They took my beautiful spleen to sell it at an inflated price and they've dumped me with a floppy, old shrunken spleen. . . ."

"We've seen signs," said Aunt Miranda, "shifty glances between doctors and nurses that speak louder than words about this conspiracy."

Uncle Joseph and Aunt Miranda had visited every ward like this, feeling patients' stomachs. They eventually left, like two incompetent detectives, in search of witnesses to and proof of this trafficking.

Happy to see his ward restored to its usual calm, Antoine turned to the suicidal woman. But her eyes were closed. A doctor came in and, talking more like a mechanic than someone who'd taken the Hippocratic oath, told Antoine he could leave the hospital.

———————

A few days went by before Antoine made up his mind to look at the piece of paper upon which the telephone number for the suicide course was written. The sun was shining on Paris at last. Exhaust pipes diffused their pollutants like the pollen of a new era, sowing the future flora of a sickly civilization in the lungs of Parisians and tourists alike. The slow death of vegetation, of the trees and flowers—so silent and invisible to those who see only moving things—was becoming the norm in this life. Cars continued to invent a new breed of man who would no longer have legs to travel through his tarmacked dreams . . . but wheels.

Antoine didn't have a telephone, so he went to the phone booth on the street corner. It was opposite the baker's shop; the warm smell of brioche erased the more unpleasant odors in the area. Antoine had to wait awhile for the booth to be free.

"SFABAM, Suicide for All by Any Means, good morning, Julie speaking, can I help you?" announced a young woman in a singsong voice.

"Hello, um, I got your number from a friend, and I'd be interested in your classes."

A tramp had huddled against the ventilation grille outside the baker's. He unwrapped a hunk of stale bread from inside a sock and bit into it as he inhaled the warm, sweet smell of Viennese pastries, mingling them with the cardboard-flavored bread in his mouth.

"In that case, sir, I recommend that you come and see us right away. There's no class this week following Professor Edmond's superb hanging, but on Monday we will have a new instructor, a woman, Professor Astanavis. I'll give you the times. Do you have pen and paper?"

"Just a moment. . . . Yes, go ahead."

"Monday to Friday, from six o'clock till eight o'clock, at number seven, Place Clichy. Just ring the bell. It's on the ground floor. There's a sign."

The following Monday Antoine stood facing the building on the Place Clichy. Among the plaques for doctors, drama lessons, a branch of Alcoholics Anonymous, a scout group, and a political party, he found a copper plaque engraved with the words SFABAM, FOUNDED 1742. Antoine pressed the button that released the latch on the heavy door to the building. He followed the signs down a corridor, then went through a pair of double doors into a long room lit by tall windows.

There were already about thirty people there.

Some were sitting down, reading or just waiting, but most were talking in little scattered groups. A quartet was playing a piece by Schubert. A tall woman dressed in a dinner jacket seemed to be in charge. She greeted Antoine affably and introduced herself as Professor Astanavis. Those attending were young, old, from all walks of life and of all sorts. They seemed relaxed, delving into their bags, chatting, exchanging articles of interest. They started to sit down. Most of them had a pad or notebook. They were waiting, pen in hand, for the class to begin, whispering and stifling quiet fits of laughter.

The room was filled with about ten rows of fifteen chairs; at the far end, on a platform, there was a desk and it was here that Professor Astanavis settled herself. All the pupils were now seated. The four walls of the room were covered with portraits or photographs of famous people who had committed suicide: Gérard de Nerval, Marilyn Monroe, Gilles Deleuze, Stefan Zweig, Mishima, Henri Roorda, Ian Curtis, Romain Gary, Hemingway, and Dalida.

The audience crackled with talk and laughter as it would before any class or conference. Antoine sat down in one of the middle rows, between an elegant man with an inscrutable face and two smiling young women. The professor coughed into her fist. Everyone fell silent.

"Ladies and gentlemen, first and foremost I

would like to announce, although some of you may already know, the success of Professor Edmond's suicide. He did it!"

Professor Astanavis took a remote control and pointed it toward a wall masked by a white screen. The image of a man hanging in a hotel room appeared. What was more, his wrists had been slashed, and the blood had made two big red circles on the beige carpet. The body must have been swinging slightly when the photo was taken because the face was out of focus. The spectators around Antoine clapped and made eulogistic comments to one another about this combination suicide.

"He did it! And, as you can see, to be doubly sure, as a security measure in case the rope snapped, he slit his wrists. I think that deserves a bit more applause!"

The pupils clapped again, stood up, cheered and whistled. Antoine stayed sitting, amazed by this demonstration of jubilation celebrating a man's death.

"We have a new friend this evening," said the professor, pointing to Antoine. "I'm going to ask him to introduce himself."

Everyone turned to look at Antoine. Feeling somewhat intimidated by the idea of speaking in public, he stood up under the well-meaning gaze and the silent encouragement of the audience.

"My name's Antoine. I . . . I'm twenty-five."

"Good evening, Antoine!" the pupils chorused.

"Antoine," the professor intervened, "can you tell us why you're here?"

"My life's a disaster," Antoine explained, still standing and nervously twiddling his hands. "But that's not the worst of it. The real problem is that I'm so aware of it. . . ."

"And you've chosen to commit suicide," murmured the professor, resting her hands on the desk, "to slip into the peace of the abyss."

"Actually, I've got so little gift for living that I thought I might be more fulfilled in death. I'll probably be better at being dead than alive."

"I'm quite sure, Antoine," the professor said, nodding, "that you'll have a very successful death. And that's why I'm here: to teach you, Antoine, and all of you, to finish with this life, which takes so much from us and gives us so little in return. My theory . . . my theory is that it's better to die before life's taken everything from you. You have to keep some ammunition, some energy, for your death so that when you get there you're not empty, not bitter and unhappy like certain old folks. It doesn't matter to me whether you're a believer, an atheist, an agnostic, or a diabetic, that's none of my business. I have certain ideas and I'm going to talk to you about them, but I'm not here to persuade you to die or to tell you about what life or death can mean. It's your experience, you have your reasons and you make your choices. What we have in common is the fact that life doesn't satisfy us and that we want to finish with it, that's all. I'm going to teach you how to commit suicide efficiently, so that you don't fail, and in a beautiful and original way. My teaching is concerned with the way in which you take your life, not the reasons why. We are not a church or a sect. Whenever you feel like it you can cry, leave the room, shout out: you have the right to do all that. You could even fall in love with the person next to you and find a new appetite for life. . . . Why not, it would allow you some good times, even if it means risking meeting me again in six months' time. If, by some misfortune, I'm still here."

Some of the people near Antoine laughed. The professor spoke calmly, not like a political or religious orator, but with all the assurance of a professor of literature before an attentive lecture theater. With her hands tucked into her dinner jacket, she was so sober in her brilliance that she had no need for exaggeration, theatrical gestures, or rhetoric as artificial means of creating emphasis.

"There is censure against suicide. Political, religious, social, even natural censure, because Mother Nature doesn't like us taking liberties with her, she wants to keep us in her clutches to the very end, she wants to decide for us. Who decides about our death? We've delegated that supreme freedom to illness, accidents, and crime. We call it fate. But that's wrong. This so-called fate is the subtle will of society, which gradually poisons us with its pollution, massacring us with wars and accidents. . . . This is how society determines the dates of our deaths from what we eat, how dangerous our daily environment is, and from our work and living conditions. We don't choose to live, we don't choose what language we speak, what country or what age we live in, what tastes we have, we don't choose our lives. Our only freedom is death; to be dead is to be free."

The professor drank a little water. She stood, leaning her hands on the edge of the desk. She looked attentively at everyone in the room, nodded with an air of complicity, as if some intimacy, some under-standing, connected them.

"But all this is hogwash. It's only later that you get to the point where you think this, where you find some kind of nobility, a legitimacy, something sublime and transcendent . . . I don't know . . . the illusion of an absolute, an absolute called death or freedom that you try to bring together in equal measures. The truth . . . my truth—and let me make this clear, I speak for myself here—is that I am unwell. There's a cancer that has decided my body makes a great paradise island, so it's spending its vacation in me, dabbling its feet in the ocean of my bloodstream, tanning itself in the sunshine of my heart. . . . It doesn't need a parasol, it couldn't give a damn about sunburn. It's getting paid leave to see that I die. I'm really suffering. . . . You all know what I'm talking about. In order to get through the day without doubling up in pain I have to have intravenous morphine, to stuff myself with painkillers." From her inside pocket she produced a little box of pills and rattled it.

"All this has a price; it will cost me my conscious mind. It's still intact at the moment but that's unlikely to last, so I'd rather extinguish myself while I'm still me rather than be unplugged by some doctor when I'm lying unconscious in a hospital bed. It's a small freedom, a pitiful one. The fact that you are here means you, too, probably have physical cancers or cancers of the soul, emotional tumors, leukemias in love and social metastases eating away at you. And that's what dictates our choice, way before any grand ideas about freedom. Let's be frank: if we were well, if we were loved as we deserve to be, respected, with a nice sunny spot within society, I'm sure this room would be empty."

The professor finished her presentation. The whole audience clapped; the two women next to Antoine stood up, affected and moved by what she had said. The professor took the red flower from her buttonhole and put it in the glass of water on the desk.

Over the next hour and a half the professor gave
her lesson. She taught several ways of committing
suicide effectively. She instructed her audience on
how to make a proper slipknot, in all its elegance and
reliability; told them which medications to choose,
what doses to take, and how to combine them in
order to die pleasantly. She dictated and prepared
recipes for beautifully colored lethal cocktails, which
she assured them were quite delicious. She detailed
different firearms and their effects on the bones of
the skull and the anatomy of the brain, depending on
the caliber and the range; recommended that before
attempting to shoot themselves in the head, subjects
should have their heads x-rayed to determine exactly
where to put the barrel to guarantee success. Using
slides of annotated diagrams, she taught her attentive pupils which blood vessels to cut in the wrist,
how to cut them, and with what. She advised against
using woollier methods such as gassing. She talked
them through famous suicides: Mishima, Cato,
Empedocles, Zweig . . . Each of these suicides was a
response to a situation, and made its own meaning
clear to the world. Finally, she ended the lesson with
an homage to Professor Edmond, reminding her
listeners that it was advisable to combine two lethal
methods to guarantee success: medication and hanging, slashed wrists and firearms.

When the lesson was over Antoine left the room

before anyone tried to start talking to him. The quartet was playing again. On his way out he passed the association's little shop with its ravishing doll's house display offering beautiful ropes, brochures, books, weapons, poisons, and dried death cap mushrooms as well as everything you might need to enjoy your death: wine, fine food, and music. He went back up the avenue de Clichy to La Fourche *métro* station; the city swam before his eyes as if he were drunk. Now that he knew how to kill himself, now that he had lost his innocence as an amateur and was in possession of a professional's knowledge, he no longer wanted to.

Antoine didn't want to live, that much was sure, but he didn't want to die, either.

"I don't know if you've noticed, but if you take the dimensions, the circumference, and the weight of a baguette, you get the golden section. And it's probably not by chance."

The baker smiled vacantly and handed him his whole wheat loaf.

———

Antoine lived in Montreuil, on the outskirts of Paris. Aaslee would say that he lived in the petticoats of Paris. Aaslee was his best friend. Antoine hardly ever used his whole name, preferring the abbreviation Aas. It made them laugh because in Samoan—and Aaslee was Samoan—it meant "water of the mountains," but it also sounded like the French word for *ace,* and Antoine was well aware that to the English-speaking world (and that's a lot of people) it sounded like the bit of you that you sit on.

Aas must have been more than six feet six inches tall but he moved with all the fluid grace of a cetacean in water. And he was blessed with a remarkable personality, which dated back to his childhood.

Major corporations tend to test new products on

panels of consumers before putting them on the market. Aaslee's parents were very poor, and they had
signed him up for tests in exchange for food vouchers. At the time, one such company had wanted to
launch a new variety of baby food with added vita-
mins and phosphorous. In tiny doses, phosphorous is
good for the health, but the quantities were bungled
at the factory when one of the engineers mistook
micrograms for kilograms. Not all the children tested
died following this industrial slipup: the survivors
suffered from various cancers and other serious illnesses. Aaslee was relatively lucky in having only
mental problems that distorted the way in which his
brain developed. Strictly speaking, he didn't have
any intellectual deficiency; it was just that his mind
went about things in its own particular way, his
reasoning followed a logic no one else could see.
Another consequence of this baby food with its ex-
cessive dose of phosphorous was that Aaslee glowed
in the dark. It was very fetching. When Aas and
Antoine walked around the city together at night,
Aas was like a huge firefly lighting their way in the
smaller unlit streets.

In order to treat his problems, Aas had spent his
childhood in special institutions. For many years he
had failed to speak and no standard methods of
speech therapy succeeded in drawing him out of his
silence. Then a speech therapist with a soft spot for

poetry discovered that he could get Aas to speak, but only in verse. His handicapped language needed feet on which to stand: the verses acted as crutches for his words. He was gradually able to return to an almost normal life, and he left the hospital when he was sixteen. Since then, despite his placid nature—he was more like a great big teddy bear than an effective deterrent—he had worked as a security guard; his impressive height was supposed to scare off potential thieves. Two other characteristics had some effect on the few burglars he did confront: first, the way he glowed caused him to look like a ghost or some sort of supernatural apparition; second, if the burglar had neither fainted nor fled, the fact that Aaslee spoke in verse finished the job of terrifying him off. For two and a half years he had been the guard at the National Museum of Natural History at the Jardin des Plantes.

That was where Antoine had met him. At the end of his shift Aas liked walking the floors of the large gallery devoted to evolution. It's a remarkable place, populated by thousands of stuffed animals, so that the visitor feels he or she is walking through a Noah's ark that has been frozen in time. A sense of mystery hangs in the air in this dimly lit place; in contrast to the lights focused onto the animals, the curious onlookers are enveloped in a shadowy half-light as they murmur and whisper to one another for fear of waking the elephant, the big cats, and the birds. One morning Antoine visited the gallery for the first time, walking up and down in a state of complete wonderment and impatience, admiring the animals captured in extraordinary poses and reading the signs that described their lives and their habitats. As he browsed, his voracious mind fed off all this knowledge on offer. His attention was drawn to a vague form that was oddly lit. At first he thought that it represented a sort of Neanderthal man or an extremely rare example of a hairless yeti that some-one had seen fit to give clothes and shoes. Antoine looked down, hoping to find an explanatory sign, a scientific note about the origins and the era of this strange specimen. He looked by the creature's feet but found nothing. He looked back up: the creature smiled at him and held out its huge hand. That was how they became friends.

They were always together. Aas didn't speak very much but that suited Antoine, whose thoughts and words were always on the move. Aas would interrupt his endless interrogations with alexandrines, and these elegant interventions with their twelve-beat rhythm covered greater expanses of meaning than all Antoine's verbosity. Antoine liked the succinct poetic nature of Aas's words, and Aas, in turn, liked the teaming jungle of Antoine's words.

Charlotte, Ganja, Rodolphe, Aas, and Antoine

met up in the evenings at Gudmundsdottir, the little
Icelandic bar on the rue Rambuteau. They played
chess and chatted, they had drinks, and they ate
dishes with unpronounceable names and mysterious
ingredients. They didn't know what they were eating, whether it was meat or fish or some extraordinary vegetable, but the peculiar flavors tickled their
palates. This little restaurant-bar was a meeting
place for expatriate Icelanders, so all the customers
gobbled in the same strange language. Antoine had
commented that here at least it was quite logical not
to understand what people were saying. He and his
friends met in this improbable place several times a
week and played Chinese Portraits, Inventing New
Countries, and a game they called Splitting the
World in Two. This consisted of finding the true
great divisions in our world, those that really matter,
because the world always, infallibly, can be split in
two: those who like going for a leisurely bicycle ride
and those who like driving fast in cars; those who
wear their shirts outside their pants and those who
tuck them in; those who take their tea with sugar
and those who take it without; those who think
Shakespeare was the greatest writer of all time and
those who think André Gide was; those who like *The
Simpsons* and those who like *South Park;* those who
like Nutella and those who like Brussels sprouts.
With genuine anthropological interest, they com-

posed these lists of the fundamental divisions within mankind.

It was during one of their secret meetings, on Thursday, July 20, one week after he left the hospital, that Antoine announced to his friends his plan to become stupid.

The restaurant was fill-ing up. A miniature Viking came out of the clock hanging on the wall and struck ten blows on a shield with his ax. The sea of Icelandic conversation and traditional music formed a little island of the table where Antoine sat with his friends. The smell of food and beer mingled, creating a mist that hung in the air in the small restaurant. Lanterns made to look like monsters and gods from Icelandic mythology shone above the customers' heads. The frantic wait-ers slalomed among the tightly packed, heavily laden tables. Antoine reached into his bag and took out the book in which he had written his profession of faith. He asked his friends not to interrupt him and—in an intense, emotional voice—he began to read:

There are people in this life for whom even the best of things don't work out. They could wear cashmere suits and still look like tramps; be very rich but badly in debt; be tall but lousy at basket-ball. I now realize that I'm one of that species who can't get the best from their advantages in life, for whom those advantages are even a drawback.

*They say "Out of the mouths of babes comes
the truth." At grade school it was the most mon-
strous insult to be called a nerd; later on being an
intellectual almost becomes a strength. But it's
a lie: intelligence is a flaw. Just as every living
person knows they're going to die while the dead
know nothing. . . .*

*It says in Ecclesiastes: "He that increaseth
knowledge increaseth sorrow"; but I never knew
the joys of going to catechism with the other kids
so I was never warned of the dangers of studying.
Christians are really very lucky being put on
their guard like that against the risks of intelligence at such an early age; they'll know to steer
clear of it all through life. Happy are the simple
of mind.*

*Those who think there's some sort of nobility
in intelligence clearly don't have enough to realize that it's a curse. My family and friends, my
classmates, my teachers, everyone's always said
I was intelligent. I've never really understood
why or how they came to that conclusion about
me. I've frequently suffered from this flattering
presumption, made by those who confuse the
appearance of intelligence with intelligence,
and condemn you for this wrongfully favorable
assessment that's put me in a position of author-
ity. Just as when the most beautiful young men*

and women are exalted, much to the quiet humiliation of others with inferior physical gifts, I've been exalted as an intelligent and cultivated creature. How much I've hated those discussions when I've contributed, despite myself, to the injury and debasement of boys and girls considered less brilliant!

I've never been athletic; the last time my muscles were tested by a major competition was playing marbles in recess at grade school. My skinny arms, my lack of fitness, and my sluggish legs meant I couldn't get together enough force to kick a ball effectively; the only thing I had the strength to do was to scour this world with my mind. I was too puny for sport. Intelligence was a fallback option.

Intelligence is one of evolution's failures. In the days of the first prehistoric humans I can just imagine some little tribe where all the kids run through the scrub chasing lizards and picking berries for their dinner; they gradually learn from the adults how to be perfect men and women: hunters, gatherers, fishermen, tanners. But if we look more closely at the life of this tribe we'll see that some children don't join in the group activities: they stay sitting by the fire, sheltered inside the cave. They'll never learn to defend themselves against a saber-toothed tiger, or how to hunt; by

*themselves they wouldn't survive a single night.
And it's not out of laziness, no, they'd like to be
capering about with their friends, but they can't.
When nature brought them into the world, it
slipped up. Within that tribe there's a little blind
girl, a boy with a limp, another one who's clumsy
and absentminded. . . . So they stay by the fire all
day and, as they've got nothing to do and video
games haven't been invented yet, they just have
to think and to let their thoughts do the capering.
So they spend all their time thinking and trying
to decipher the world, dreaming up stories and
making inventions. That's how civilization was
born: because a bunch of imperfect kids had
nothing better to do. If nature never maimed
anyone, if the mold was always flawless, the human race would have stayed a protohominid
species, quite happy with no thoughts of progress,
living perfectly well without Prozac or condoms
or Dolby digital DVDs.*

    *To be curious, to strive to understand the
nature and humanity, to discover the arts—this
should be the tendency of every soul. But if that
were the case, with the current system of employment, the world would stop spinning, simply
because it would take time and increase the
amount of general criticism. No one would work
any more. Because people have their likes and*

dislikes, the things that interest them and the things that don't; because, if not, we wouldn't have a society. Those who are interested in too many things, those who are interested in things they don't find inherently interesting—and those who want to understand their reasons for disinterest—pay the price with a certain type of solitude. In order to escape this ostracism, it's necessary to equip oneself with one type of intelligence, one with a singular function, one that's useful to a specific scientific field or to one cause, one trade; in essence, an intelligence that's useful for something. My presumed intelligence, too independent in its nature, isn't useful for anything, i.e. it can't be turned into a position at a university, a company, a magazine, or a law firm.

I have the curse of reason: I'm poor, single, and depressed. For months now I've been thinking about my illness of thinking too much, and I've established with complete certainty the correlation between my unhappiness and the incontinence of my mind. Probing and pondering and overanalyzing have never given me any advantages; they've only played against me. The process of thought is not a natural one, it hurts; it's as if I were uncovering pieces of broken glass and lengths of barbed wire in the air. I can't seem to stop my brain or to slow it down. I feel like a *train, a big old steam train hurtling along the tracks, a train that will never be able to stop because the fuel that makes it so dizzyingly powerful, the coal, is the whole world. Everything I see, feel, and hear throws itself into the furnace of my mind, fires it up and makes it charge on full steam ahead. Probing and pondering and over-analyzing is a kind of social suicide because it means you can no longer take part in this life without inadvertently feeling both like a bird of prey and a vulture picking apart everything it sees. When we try to understand something, more often than not we kill it, and now I can feel the dangers of this encroaching on me: cynicism, bitterness, and infinite sadness. You very quickly become good at being unlucky and unhappy. It's impossible to live if you're too aware, too thoughtful. Take nature, for example: everything that lives happily and to a ripe old age is not very intelligent. Tortoises live for centuries, water's immortal, and Milton Friedman's still alive. In nature, awareness is an exception; you could even postulate that it's an accident because it gives no guarantee of superiority or of particular longevity. In the context of the evolution of species, it doesn't represent any better form of adaptation. In terms of age, numbers, and occupied territories, insects are actually the masters of the planet. For example, the social structure of an ant colony is far more effective than ours will ever be, and there isn't a single ant with a chair at Harvard.*

Everyone's got something to say about women, men, the police, *and* murderers. *We generalize according to our own experiences, to suit ourselves, depending on what we understand within the slender means of our neuronal networks and in the context of our perception of things. This faculty enables us to think quickly, judge, and take a position. It has no intrinsic value, it's just a system of signals, of little flags we all wave. And everyone defends the virtues of their own advantages, their sex, and their lot in life.*

In a debate, generalization has the advantage of simplicity and of making arguments more fluid so that they're readily understandable, therefore they have greater impact on the listener. To translate that into mathematical terms, discussions based on generalizations are like additions, simple operations that are so self-evident they seem convincing and relevant. On the other hand, a serious discussion would seem more like a succession of inequations containing several unknowns, integrals, and reshufflings of complex numbers.

A learned person taking part in a discussion

will think they're simplifying things, and all they really want is to make deletions and alterations, sticking asterisks at the ends of words, putting footnotes at the bottom of the page and endnotes at the end of the book to explain what they're really thinking, and from where it stems. But in a casual conversation at the end of a corridor, at a sparkling dinner party, or in the columns of a newspaper, that can't really happen: there's no room for rigorous accuracy, objectivity, impartiality, or honesty. Virtue is a rhetorical handicap, completely inefficient in a debate.

Men simplify the world with words and thoughts, and that's how they create their certainties; and having certainty is the most potent pleasure in this world, far more potent than money, sex, and power all combined. Renouncing true intelligence is the price we have to pay for having these certainties, and it's an expenditure that never gets noticed by the bank of our minds. In this instance, I actually prefer those who don't huddle behind the cloak of reason, and come out and admit the illusory nature of their beliefs. Like a believer admitting that his faith is just his own belief and not preemption on the truths of this world.

There's a Chinese proverb that goes something along these lines: a fish never knows when it's pissing. The same applies perfectly well to intellectuals. An intellectual is convinced of his own intelligence because he's using his brain. A mason uses his hands, but he too has a brain that can say, "Hey! That wall's not straight and, anyway, you've forgotten to put the cement between the breeze blocks." There's a dialogue between his hands at work and his mind. The intellectual who works within his mind doesn't have that dialogue; his hands don't pipe up and say, "Come on, man, you've really goofed up! The Earth is round." The intellectual doesn't have that distance, that discrepancy, so he thinks he has or can have an enlightened view on every subject.

Intellectuals obviously aren't the only people concerned with intelligence. In general, when someone begins by saying, "I don't mean to be pedantic . . ." it is precisely in order to be pedantic. Thus, I don't know how to say anything that could be interpreted as condescension. I'm convinced that intelligence is a virtue shared by the totality of the population, without any social distinctions: there's the same percentage of intelligent people amongst history teachers and Breton sea fishermen, amongst writers and typists. That comes from my experience, from rubbing elbows with hungry minds, thinkers and profes-

sors, silly intellectuals, and, at the same time, with normal people, intelligent people who haven't been officially certified as such, those without the academic pedigree. I can't say anything else. It's as suspect as a scientific study is impossible—more so. To find someone intelligent, judicious—this is not the function of academia; there is no I.Q. test that reveals what might be called common sense. I recall what Michael Herr, who wrote the screenplay for Full Metal Jacket, *said in Michel Ciment's superb book about Kubrick: "People's stupidity doesn't arise from their lack of intelligence, but from the absence of courage."*

One thing that can be conceded is that, even if we get no guarantee of intelligence from familiarity with great works, using our minds and reading the work of geniuses, it does at least increase risk. Of course there will be people who've read Freud and Plato, who can juggle with quarks, and tell the difference between a peregrine falcon and a kestrel, and who'll still be idiots. All the same, by being in contact with a multitude of stimuli and by exposing the mind to an enriching environment, intelligence can potentially find a breeding ground just like any other disease. Because intelligence is a disease.

At last, Antoine had reached his conclusion. He closed his notebook and looked at his friends like an old sage who had just implacably demonstrated one of the great mysteries of science to an amazed gathering of distinguished colleagues.

G anja could not stop
laughing. An Icelander sitting at the table
behind them handed him his pack of cigarettes: apparently the quavering, bleating sound of Ganja's
laugh meant something like "Do you have any cigarettes?" in Icelandic. Every time he laughed some
kindly Icelander would offer him a cigarette.
Rodolphe pointed out that Antoine wouldn't have to
make a great deal of effort to become stupid; Charlotte took his hand affectionately; Aas just gazed at
him with his great big astonished eyes.

Antoine explained, with moving simplicity, that
he couldn't help thinking and analyzing, and that it
was making him unhappy. It was as if studying gave
him the same pleasure as searching for gold . . . But
the gold he found was the color and weight of lead.
His mind gave him no respite, stopped him from
sleeping with its endless interrogations, woke him
up in the middle of the night with its doubts and
indignations. Antoine told his friends that it was a
long time since he had had a dream or a nightmare
because his ideas took up so much space when he
was asleep. As a result of thinking so much, with his
brain constantly, tumescently aware, Antoine wasn't

really living. He now wanted to lose some of that
awareness, to become mostly ignorant of causes,
truths, and reality. He'd had enough of this acute
power of observation that drew him a cynical picture
of human relationships. He wanted to live, not *to
know the truth about life,* but just to live.

He reminded his anxious friends of his attempt
to become an alcoholic and of his aborted suicide.
Stupidity was his last chance to be saved. He still
wasn't sure how to proceed, but he promised to de-
vote every ounce of his will to becoming stupid. He
was hoping to water down his Shirley Temple, to
relax, to throw off the heavy burden that was the
truth. Antoine didn't want to be a complete idiot;
rather, he wanted to thin down his intelligence by
alloying it with a proper life, to let himself go so that
he didn't always have to analyze and get to the bottom of everything. His mind had always been an
eagle with a keen eye, a piercing beak, and sharp
talons. He now wanted to learn to be a regal crane,
gliding through the air, carried by the wind, enjoying
the beautiful countryside and the warmth of the sun.

It wasn't as if he were renouncing his powers of
reasoning gratuitously: the aim was to participate in
life as a member of society. He always tried to find the
motives and the reasons that drive each creature; he
knew just how little a part free will plays in our
choice of opinions. Part of his problem derived from

the fact that he lived under the rule of the tragedy exposed by Jean Renoir: "What creates unhappiness in this world" is the fact that "everyone has their reasons." He would apply Spinoza's formula as if it were a vocation: "not to laugh . . . not to lament . . . nor to hate . . . but to understand." He always tried not to judge, even those who wanted to hurt him and put him down. Antoine was the sort of soul who could construct a dental plate for a shark and would even try to install it in the animal's mouth. His tendency to try to understand everything had none of the religious overtones of those who go about forgiving everything so condescendingly. Beneath the varnish of freedom and choice he could see, perhaps in an exaggerated way, necessity and the mechanics of the machine feeding off human souls. At the same time—because he liked to be as objective about himself as he was about others—he saw that in trying to understand everything he had learned not to live and not to love. He realized that his extreme intellectual probity could be interpreted as a fear of engaging properly in life, as a way of carving out a little niche. He was aware of this and it contributed to his decision.

"But," he added, "the truth, like Janus, has two faces, and so far I have seen only its darker face. Now I'm going to explore its bright, sunlit face. To forget wanting to understand, to become passionate about everyday things, to believe in politics, to buy beautiful clothes, to follow big sports matches, to dream about the latest model of a car, to watch the news on TV, to dare to hate stuff . . . I haven't experienced that, being interested in everything but passionate about nothing. I'm not saying that's good or bad, just that I'm going to try and I'm going to be a part of that great mind known as 'public opinion.' I want to be *with* other people, not to understand them, but to be like them, amongst them, experiencing the same things as them . . ."

"You mean," Ganja said slowly as he chewed on some medicinal seeds, "you mean that you were stupid to try and be intelligent, that you didn't have a clue, and that becoming a bit stupid will actually be intelligent . . . ?"

"But," said Charlotte, "we really like you as you are. You're a bit complicated, but . . . you're a great guy. If I was straight . . ."

"Yeah, you know, Charlotte," Antoine replied, "if I was a Danish girl I'd ask if you'd marry me. Listen, it strikes me that a degree of antisocial behavior is about as normal as you can get; it's even good to have a few problems with society. I don't want to be completely integrated, but I don't want to be disintegrated, either."

"Have to find the right balance, man," said Ganja.

"Yes," Charlotte agreed, "or a balanced imbalance."

The waiter brought them bowls of a thick greenish soup and glasses filled with a murky liquid that had red berries rising to the surface. The five friends peered cautiously at their food. The waiter produced a great series of consonants from his throat, probably meaning something like *bon appétit*. Speaking within the constrained meter of a haiku, Aas then asked Antoine if there was any danger that he might really lose himself, and that they'd suddenly find him working as a talk-show host. Antoine replied that this was an adventure, and that great human adventures are not without their dangers: Magellan, Cook, and Giordano Bruno were all valid examples. So far he had lived in the eye of a hurricane, a quiet solitary place surrounded by an infernal storm. He wanted to leave this accursed place, to cut through the swathes of the destructive vortex and reach the secular world outside.

Antoine's friends were worried and sad for him. They comforted him, made him promise not to do anything really crazy, and managed to persuade him to go and ask for advice from his doctor and confidant, Edgar.

Dr. Edgar Vaporski's
office was on the third floor of an imposing
building in the Twentieth Arrondissement of Paris,
on the rue des Pyrénées, just by the Place Gambetta.
Antoine had been coming to him since the age of
two, and had never seen another doctor.

He was a pediatrician, but no one knew Antoine
better than he did. As they had known each other
for twenty-three years, there was a degree of intimacy
between them: they were on first-name terms and
they occasionally went out together in the evenings
because they shared a passion for the Brady, an old
cinema on the boulevard de Strasbourg.

From about the age of twenty Antoine had
grown increasingly embarrassed at being the only
adult not accompanied by a child sitting patiently
in the waiting room. Parents would watch Antoine
discreetly over the tops of their magazines, and their
little ones stared at him openly. However cleverly
he sat himself next to single women, the revelation of
his nonownership of a child eventually erupted. That
was why he had taken to borrowing his neighbor's
grandson—or any other available child—every
time he went. On that particular day he had dragged

along little Coralie, the daughter of the concierge in his building, and she was not demonstrating a great deal of enthusiasm for providing him with an alibi.

Edgar opened the door to his waiting room, complete with surgeon's mask over his face. He called Antoine and Coralie into his office. The room looked like any other doctor's office with its diplomas hanging on the beige-colored walls, its bookcase of hefty volumes magnificently bound in the hide of a cow that must have grazed on solid gold. As if the copper plaque by the door were not enough, the whole office exuded a certified aura of competence; the colors and the furniture created a feeling of gravitas. Anyone who set foot in the place was assailed by the atmosphere of solemnity, felt the monarchial presence of Medicine the all-powerful, and had no choice but to submit to it. Going to the doctor very often forces us to abandon any power we may have over ourselves: we no longer really belong to ourselves, we offer up our bodies and their dysfunctions to the sorcery of medical science. The similarities between the knick-knacks you find in every doctor's office and those that create the air of mystery in the rooms of a medium or a witch doctor are quite astonishing. Anyone with a mischievous, critical mind might be tempted to draw comparisons between the two settings: even at the level of the smell of medicinal products and the smell of incense, there's a sense of a shared intention, a similar attempt to influence the client's perceptions. But Edgar's office didn't quite fall into that trap because there were children's drawings on the walls, and scribbles, toys, and plasticine were scattered over the floor and the desk. A red Power Ranger standing on Edgar's prescription pad defused the symbolic power of his standing as a doctor.

The window was open, and a slight smell of tear gas hung in the air. That explained Edgar's mask, which he promptly removed now that the air was breathable again. Antoine commented on the smell, while Coralie pulled a face and pinched her nose.

"A kind of unruly ten-year-old boy, he tried to steal my prescriptions."

"You used tear gas on him for that?" Antoine asked indignantly.

"He had nunchakus," explained Edgar, raising his hands helplessly. "Nunchakus, Antoine!"

"My God, does that happen a lot?"

"No, I'm happy to say. Hello, Coralie," Edgar said, having sat down behind his desk. "Is it for you or for Antoine?"

"It's for him," Coralie replied reproachfully. "At his age he still needs me to go to the doctor with him!"

"I do pay you, Coralie," said Antoine. "And not badly."

"Two chocolate croissants and a copy of *Première* magazine . . . I should look into raising my rates. I mean, inflation has to affect human relationships too."

"Coralie, does your mother let you read the financial pages of newspapers? That's incredible."

"You'll have to get used to it, it's the new generation. So, Antoine, what's going on?"

Antoine rummaged through the hodgepodge of books, newspapers, and scraps of paper in his bag, and produced a photocopied diagram of the human brain in cross section. He laid it down on the desk, picked up Edgar's Montblanc pen, and pointed out the areas of the brain.

"The higher cognitive functions are taken care of by the cortex of the neo-cerebrum, right?"

"Yes . . . What have you gone and done this time? What are you getting at? Have you decided to become a neurosurgeon?"

"The frontal lobes, here," Antoine went on, circling the relevant areas, "deal with communication between the structures of the self and the cognitive functions. . . ."

"That's very good, Antoine. I'm a doctor, you're not telling me anything new. We know all that."

"Okay," said Antoine, still concentrating on his diagram, "I wondered whether you could remove some of the cortex, or, if you prefer, get rid of a frontal lobe, like this . . ."

Edgar watched, perplexed, as Antoine scribbled out the parts of his brain that could be removed. His eyebrows slowly furrowed as he stared at his friend and patient. Coralie was reading her film magazine on the couch at the far end of the office.

"What in the name of God are you talking about?" Edgar asked, jumping to his feet. "I'm not following you. Have you lost the plot, are you completely stupid, or what?"

"That's what I'd like," Antoine replied very seriously. "That's the aim of all this. I . . ."

"You want me to perform a lobotomy on you?" Edgar interrupted him, terrified.

"Actually I think a half-lobotomy would be enough: I still want to able to strike a match and open my icebox; I'm not talking *One Flew Over the Cuckoo's Nest* here. . . . Anyhow, you're the doctor, you do what you think is best."

"What would be best would be to shut you up in a nuthouse. What's happened to you?"

"No, no, it's not what you think. . . . I'm asking you this with a perfectly clear head and in possession of all my faculties. I'll sign a disclaimer. I've thought about this a lot. I'm making this decision with my soul and my conscience. It wasn't my first choice,

I'll tell you that right away; first I wanted to become an alcoholic, then I tried suicide, but they didn't work out."

"You wanted to commit suicide?"

"Disastrous. I don't want to talk about it."

Edgar came round his desk and sat down next to Antoine. He put one hand on Antoine's shoulder, filled with concern for this his best known, closest patient, his friend.

"Are you depressed? Is there something wrong?" he asked anxiously.

"Everything's wrong, Edgar. But don't worry about it, I'm looking for a solution right now. I think the best thing would be to become stupid."

"What?"

"Would you do me a favor? Describe me. If you had to tell someone about me, what would you say?"

"I don't know. . . . That you're brilliant, intelligent, cultured, curious (in both senses of the word), friendly, amusing, a bit disorganized and indecisive, anxious . . ."

As the pediatrician listed the qualities that characterized his friend, Antoine's face darkened as if it were a list of serious illnesses afflicting him.

"That's an exaggeratedly flattering portrait, but truth be told, my life is hell. I know plenty of people who are really dumb, ignorant, stuffed full of prejudices and ideas, complete morons, and they're happy! But I'll soon have an ulcer, I already have a few gray hairs. . . . I don't want to go on living like this, I can't. I've studied my case endlessly and I've deduced that my poor social adaptability is all due to my sulfuric intelligence. It never gives me a moment's peace. If I don't master it it's going turn me into one of those creepy, haunted manor houses, a dark, dangerous, scary place, possessed by my tormented spirit. I'm haunting myself."

"Even if your intelligence is the cause of all your problems, I can't do what you're asking. As a doctor, I just can't, it's completely unethical. And as a friend, I don't want to."

"Ed, you've got to help me, I can't take any more of this thinking. My brain's running a marathon all day and all night, it never stops turning—like a hamster's wheel, it just keeps going and going."

"I'm really sorry, I can't. I don't understand you: you're fantastic, unique, you've no idea how lucky you are. You'll have to learn to live as who you are. But for now, just as long as it takes for you to get better, to get the upper hand, we'll find a solution to help you along, to improve your life."

"My life would improve if I were stupid."

"That's stupid."

"I'm on the right track, then. Couldn't I have

some of my neurons removed? There are organ
banks, blood banks, sperm banks; there must be
neuron banks, too, aren't there? That way, anyone
who has too many neurons can give some to those
who have a deficiency. It would be a humanitarian
gesture as well."

"No, there's no such thing, Antoine. I'm really
sorry."

"What can you do, then, Ed? What's going to
happen to me? Why am I different? I want an ordinary life, I want to conform. I want to be an ant, just
another ant along with all the other ants."

As he talked Antoine doodled on the cross section of a brain; he drew ants all round the illustra-
tion, and one bigger ant that was supposed to
represent him.

"Do you remember the book you gave me for my
tenth birthday?"

"*Mr. Bumpsadaisy*?"

"Yes, *Mr. Bumpsadaisy*. Whatever he does,
everything always goes wrong for him: when he goes
out it rains, he knocks his head on things all the time,
he leaves the cake in the oven, loses all his stuff,
always misses his bus . . . Why? Because he's Mr.
Bumpsadaisy! Edgar, I feel like I'm turning into Mr.
Bumpsadaisy. . . . Mr. Bumpsadaisy, that's me!"

There were tears streaming down Antoine's

cheeks. Edgar embraced him and patted him gently on the shoulder, which set him off on a long paroxysm of coughing. Edgar took a bottle of syrup from a drawer; he gave two spoonfuls to Antoine and then offered him a Twix. Antoine bit into the chocolate bar voraciously; his eyes were now dry and he was gradually calming down.

"Have you thought about going to an analyst?"

"I've been to an analyst," Antoine said helplessly, spreading his hands.

"And?"

"He says all this is perfectly normal: I don't have any psychological pathology, or any . . . Do you know what he said to me? He said: 'Make the most of life, young man, relax. Stop worrying.' What kind of school of psychiatry did he go to to say a thing like that? The School of Tomjonesian thinking?"

"Right. What I would suggest," said the doctor, "is that I prescribe you some Happyzac. Usually, I'm against that kind of medication, but given your attempted suicide, attempted alcoholism, and your general state, I'm forced to resort to this option. Although it won't resolve anything, really, and it doesn't cure you, it is a quick fix."

"I just want to think less, Ed."

"Happyzac has a tranquilizing, antidepressant effect. It's exactly what you need. It does have some

79

risks, and that's why I'd like you to come and see me every month to see whether or not I should repeat the prescription."

"Some risks—what do you mean?"

"The usual little side effects of medication: dryness of the mucous membrane, possible dizziness, fatigue . . . and, a very pleasant dependence. You must be sure to read the instructions on the pamphlet and to take the correct dose."

"And with these I'll think less?" Antoine asked hopefully.

"You'll practically be a zombie, I can guarantee it. Life will seem simpler, more beautiful. Which won't be true, of course, but you won't know that. You have to realize that this can only be short-term."

"That's fine," Antoine reassured him. "You know, you're right, it's better not to do something too definitive. I let myself get a bit carried away. I see this as a sort of buoy, you know. It'll help me stay afloat for a while, then I'll be able to look after myself."

They carried on chatting for a few minutes, about their respective families, their friends, and about movies. Antoine often had questions for Edgar, questions that he felt would be within the scope of his medical competence: why fizzy drinks make you burp, why nails grow, why we sneeze, why we get hiccups, why when you scratch chalk down the blackboard or a fork across a plate the sound is so grating. With the

proposed treatment noted and the prescription made
out, Edgar and Antoine shook hands warmly. As
usual, Antoine wanted to pay for the consultation,
and, as usual, Edgar refused. Coralie and Antoine left
the doctor's office.

H is studio was on the eighth floor of an old building in Montreuil. During grade school and high school, Antoine—along with the other children not cut out for physical education activities—had suffered that institutionalized humiliation of always being among the last to be chosen to make up a team for football or volleyball. He had had to put up with the angry slurs and vicious teasing of classmates who saw physical education lessons as having nothing to do with exercise and fun, and everything to do winning. Antoine had, therefore, developed little taste for sports. But it annoyed him that he had succumbed to this negative experience and exercise, so he had decided to rent a studio on one of the higher floors, which would force him—in theory—to use his muscles. In practice, this quickly turned out to be too exhausting. His downstairs neighbor on the seventh floor was a champion wrestler, a kind man by the name of Vlad. Given that he was permanently in training, lifting weights and doing toning exercises, he offered to carry Antoine as far as his floor. So Antoine always tried to arrive at the bottom of the staircase at the same time as him, so that Vlad could carry him over his shoulder up to the

seventh floor. According to Vlad, Antoine didn't
weigh any more than a hand towel, so it was fine, as
long as Vlad didn't try to dry himself off with Antoine after a shower. Vlad was six feet tall and must
have weighed 260 pounds; he was so strong that he
had once forgotten Antoine was on his shoulder, gone
into his apartment, and started cooking his supper.

Antoine's studio was not exactly chic; in fact it
was pretty dilapidated: the radiators, the insulation,
the plumbing, the electricity . . . nothing worked
properly. But it was still way beyond Antoine's
means. At first he had managed to pay the rent
thanks to a student allowance and to his income
from translating Proust's *In Search of Lost Time*
into Aramaic. But since that project had been abandoned, following the publisher's devastating bank-
ruptcy, his finances had been at an all-time low. As
he watched his wallet agonizing on its deathbed he
had pictured a financial hospital where anemic bank
accounts could be given transfusions. Antoine had
talked about this to his bank manager, but the latter
seemed to think of the bank more in terms of a pri-
vate clinic.

In search of a classification system for the human
race, Antoine had established a universal scale determining degrees of wealth measured in socks. The
first category, the poorest, had no socks; the second

category, the moderately poor, had holes in their socks; the third category, the rich, had socks without holes. Antoine was in the second category. His income derived chiefly from his sessions as a junior lecturer at Paris V, which, depending on the month, brought in between five hundred and one thousand Euros. Added to that was the welfare money that he was able to claim completely illegally thanks to some confusion about his first name: on his university documents he was Antoine Arakan, but he was registered with the unemployment agency under his Burmese name, Sawlu, which he had never used in everyday life. He also occasionally did some odd jobs under the table. Recently, for example, he had dubbed the calls of a family of giraffes in a nature documentary for which the soundtrack had been lost. His parents in Brittany sent him a little money and some food parcels. These were an astonishing and delicious mixture of Asian and Breton specialties. Every month a heavy cool box would arrive full of spring rolls filled with fish and clams, samosas of samphire, scallop dumplings, flambéed nuoc mam buckwheat pancakes stuffed with stir-fried rice. . . . His friend Ganja helped him too, and he would have helped him more if Antoine didn't refuse handouts.

Antoine survived each month on less than the

minimum wage, but he still stayed in his studio. How? He no longer paid any rent. Why? Because the landlord, Mr. Brallaire, had Alzheimer's.

Antoine was not absolutely sure that it was Alzheimer's, but in any event, Mr. Brallaire didn't remember anything. At the beginning of September Antoine had to take Mr. Brallaire to the hospital for some tests (he had no family so Antoine looked after him). It was only by chance that Antoine had noticed his amnesia at all. Antoine couldn't give him his rent money every month, so he would sneak along the walls and try to make himself as invisible as possible. All the same Mr. Brallaire caught him one day. Antoine expected him to throw him out; instead he clutched his arm and gazed at him with empty eyes, murmuring, "Do you live here?"

"Yes, sir. On the eighth floor. I'd like to apologize, this month has been a bit difficult . . . I forgot . . ."

"Have you forgotten something?" he asked with naïve, open-eyed concern.

Usually Mr. Brallaire insisted that rent payments were made on the first of the month; at precisely seven o'clock in the morning the envelope should be slipped under his door. Antoine had to be only a couple of hours late for Mr. Brallaire to hammer on his door threatening to send in the bailiffs.

"Um, no," replied Antoine, sweating. "I forgot to say hello to you. Hello . . ."

"Hello," he murmured. "Do you live in this building?"

"Yes, sir. On the eighth floor."

Now, this presented a difficult situation for Antoine's conscience. He could let the illness run its course and be free to stay on in his studio, or he could look after his landlord, who had once been ill-tempered and unfriendly. His innate kindness won the day. Antoine thought sadly that he really should be doing toning exercises on his selfishness and his amorality if he was to survive in this world.

He took him to the doctor's. The doctor delayed his diagnosis: it would take time and whole batteries of tests to identify Mr. Brallaire's illness with any certainty.

"And what are his chances of recovery?"

"That's hard to say," replied the doctor. "His memory is in shreds. You'll have to keep an eye on him. He has all his wits about him but he has absolutely no short-term memory."

Antoine looked after him as if he were an aging uncle. He took him back to his apartment when he found him wandering through the corridors; he drew a little map for him with his address on it, and slipped it into his wallet, in case he got lost in the street. He did his shopping, harvested the rent from the other tenants and put it into the old man's bank account. Mr. Brallaire still had lucid periods during which he remembered some things, particularly the fact that Antoine wasn't paying the rent; but they didn't last long. Antoine had read an article in *Le Monde* about the advances in medical research on degenerative diseases of the brain: Parkinson's, Alzheimer's . . . He was both happy for Mr. Brallaire and anxious to think that scientific advances might result in his expulsion. Scientists never think about the nonmedical consequences of their discoveries. If they ended up curing his landlord's illness, Antoine wouldn't be able to rely on his gratitude: by looking through his accounts, the old man would clearly see the rent that hadn't been paid, but he would have no memory at all of the help Antoine had given him.

The day after the consultation at Edgar's office, on Thursday, July 27, Antoine started taking the medication that was supposed to protect him from his own mind: Happyzac. The dose was one pill a day. Antoine took the initiative of doubling it. He wanted a quick and noticeable effect, not a gentle balm for some superficial result. The effects would start to show after a few days, just the time Antoine needed to organize his new life with all his ingenuity still at his disposal.

First stage: he sent a letter of resignation to the

University of Paris V René-Descartes. For two years
he had been giving a weekly ninety-minute class on
The Divine Claudius's Apocolocyntosis (his meta-
morphosis into a pumpkin, that is), a satirical play
by Seneca. He also occasionally supplied teaching in
the subjects he knew reasonably well: biology, lepi-
dopterology, Aramaic rhetoric, and film. He had
enough specialized knowledge on a good many subjects to stand in for a sick lecturer at a moment's
notice, but not the in-depth knowledge that represented a mastery of any one subject so that he might
have hoped for a permanent position.

Second stage: he got rid of everything that ran
the risk of stimulating his mind. He put his books
in cardboard boxes: the hundreds of novels, works
of theory, dictionaries and encyclopedias, his CDs,
pounds of notes taken in classes, of facts, of scientific,
historic, and literary reviews. . . . He took the film
posters down from the walls of his single room, along
with the portraits of his heroes and reproductions of
paintings by Rembrandt, Schiele, Edward Hopper,
and Miyazaki. Aas, Charlotte, Vlad, and Ganja helped
him carry the boxes to Rodolphe's apartment. The
latter was delighted to house these cultural treasures—
as Antoine had promised it wouldn't be temporary.

Third stage: with his studio empty, Antoine wondered how he'd managed to put so much stuff in such
a small space. He now had to fill it with inoffensive

things that would leave his mind in peace. After a few
self-interested visits to the apartments of a number of
neighbors whom he deemed to have excellent
immune defenses against intelligence, he made
notes on what constituted a perfect decor for his new
life. A neighboring couple—comprised of a teacher
named Alain and a journalist named Isabelle—
struck him as being an edifying example of a life
entirely devoted to a renunciation of intelligence. He
had been watching them for a long time and, deep
down, he admired them: they were so wholly
involved in life, and had so absolutely every last
nuance of a dazzling stupidity, a pure idiocy, full of
innocence, happy and replete, a lack of awareness
that was pleasant both for them and for those around
them, not in the least bit nasty or dangerous. With a
genuine sincerity that was quite charmingly ridiculous, Alain and Isabelle advised him on how to fill
his studio. He picked up an old television, which he
installed in the middle of the room as the sovereign
symbol of his resolution. He taped up posters of *The
Lion King,* sports cars, and pneumatic young
women; photographs of actors and actresses with
their penetrating, I'm-a-genius expressions, and of
immortal intellectual personalities such as Alain
Minc and Alain Finkielkraut. At first he found it
quite disturbing, and felt uncomfortable in this ster-
ile setting, but he took comfort in the fact that,

thanks to the chemistry of Happyzac, everything
would soon seem wonderful to him. Alain and
Isabelle recommended some inoffensive folk music.

At last he felt that his apartment was so perfectly
innocuous that it would assist the intended flaccidity
of his brain. Antoine did, however, realize that even
if the outside world was following the same course,
he couldn't hope to eradicate completely the slight
cultural and intellectual dangers of society.

———————

Antoine invited Charlotte, Ganja, Aas, and
Rodolphe to his newly decorated apartment for an
Icelandic tea party. The table was laden with Nordic
delicacies: tea with butter, penguin-flavored *louk-
oums,* seal-fat fritters with a confit of herbs . . . Seeing Antoine's enterprise as the least destructive, his
friends reluctantly promised him their support. Antoine asked them not to provoke him with conversation on big topics, but to chatter about one thing and
another, the weather, all those anodyne things he had
neglected until now.

"So, I guess our chess games are a thing of the
past?" asked Ganja.

"For now, yes. But we could substitute another
game that my neighbors introduced me to. It's called
Monopoly. The aim of the game is very simple: you

have to get money, be crafty with it . . . behave like the perfect, idiotic capitalist. It's fascinating. One of the virtues of the game is that it should teach me, and perhaps even convert me—in its own playful way—to a liberal-minded morality. I will adhere to something that, at the moment, I condemn as a simple game, and I won't worry about the crippling rents that put so many families out on the streets. I'll become selfish and penny-pinching, and the only thing I'll worry about will be money, the only thing that will matter to me, my only big existential question, will be how I can get as much of it as possible."

"You could wind up a real jerk, then," said Charlotte.

"Being a real jerk is a good remedy for my problem. I need a radical treatment: being a jerk will be like chemotherapy for my intelligence. And I'm prepared to take the risk without hesitation. But if, in six months' time, I seem to be enjoying myself a bit too much as a . . . as a selfish bastard, I'd like you to step in. I'm not trying to become stupid and money-grabbing; I just want to let those molecules circulate in my organism to purge this painful mind. But don't step in before six months."

In a magnificent sonnet, Aas told Antoine that he might lose his personality, that he could be contaminated by these poisons he was going to absorb into himself.

"There is a risk of that, too. Especially as being stupid makes life much better than living under the yoke of intelligence. It makes you happier for sure. I wouldn't want to keep the stupidity itself, but the many beneficial particles floating around in it like trace elements: happiness, a bit of detachment, the ability to avoid suffering by empathizing, a lightness in the way you live and think. Being carefree!"

"I understand," said Rodolphe. "I'd call it the shark theory. Like curare poison and death cap mushrooms, sharks are lethally dangerous, but in their tissues there are chemicals that we use to make medicines for curing cancers and saving lives. In fact, by becoming stupid you could prove your extraordinary intelligence once and for all. I hope that doesn't sound deceitful."

"It's also the vaccination theory," Charlotte went on. "You might succeed in curing yourself and immunizing yourself."

"If I don't die of it," said Antoine, running his hand round the back of his neck with a rather anxious smile.

"Or if you don't become irremediably stupid," said Charlotte. "Which would be worse than death."

In his naïveté, Antoine saw stupidity as a portal to a vast, infinitely happy universe: he would float among the stars and planets, following the elliptical orbit of his species.

H aving made up his

mind, now the only big problem confronting
Antoine was how to find those wonderful mines in
which the earth harbored the gems of stupidity.
Pointing a finger at the odd idiot in the street, or at
general ambient dumbness, would be easy, but it's
usually a camouflage for a value judgment. If you
could just say that football, TV game shows, and the
media are intrinsically stupid, then it would be simple. But, as far as Antoine could see, it was obvious
that stupidity lay more in the way things were done
or perceived than in the things themselves. At the
same time, having prejudices was stupid, and Antoine found that his new life was off to a good start.

The Happyzac started to have an effect. Antoine
was more relaxed, released from his doubts and anxi-
eties. The alchemy taking place within his brain and
his nervous system transformed the lead of reality
into a luminous, colorful, golden powder.

Before, he hadn't been able to live his life because of all the questions and principles tangled in
his mind. For example, when he bought clothes he
would always check where they came from so that he
wouldn't be participating in the exploitation of chil-

dren in Asian sweatshops owned by multinational
corporations. As advertising is an assault on freedom, a coup d'état on the consumer's imagination
and subconscious, he had drawn up a notebook list-
ing every brand and product that took part in this
psychological war, and he wouldn't put them any-
where near his shopping bag. He also kept a register
of every company that invested in morally reprehen-
sible activities, pollutants, or nondemocratic countries,
or who laid people off when their profits were in-
creasing. He didn't eat food full of chemicals either,
or anything containing preservatives, coloring, or an-
tioxidants, and—financial circumstances permitting—
he bought organic. It wasn't so much that he was an
ecologist, a pacifist, or even an internationalist—just
that he did what his conscience told him was right;
his behavior derived more from moral principles
than from political convictions. In that, Antoine was
not unlike a martyr of this consumer society, and he
was perfectly well aware that his intransigent attitude begged comparison with Christian mortifica-
tion. This was an embarrassment to him because he
was an atheist, but he couldn't act any other way,
he couldn't help being this sort of renegade, secular
Christ. Having always tried not to hide anything
from himself, Antoine had wondered whether this
painful, crucifying austerity was his way of express-
ing Western-male-exploiting-the-Third-World guilt.

Like any abstemious cleric, he had fairly rigid principles: he refused to fall into the trap of new technolo-
gies that periodically force consumers to reequip
themselves with the latest model. He had, therefore,
rejected CDs and made do—quite rightly—with the
technical excellence of his old record player and 33-
rpm albums.

There is unfortunately a price to pay for having a
responsible and humanist attitude as a consumer.
Antoine paid more for everything. The net result of
his morals and his acute sense of responsibility was
that he had few clothes and he was often hungry. But
he never complained.

Now, basking in the chemical sunlight of Happyzac, Antoine discovered the world. He saw it as he
had never seen it. Before, the countryside, the air, the
streets, people, everything, had been affected by
the violence of wars, by unemployment, disease, and
the daily misery of a human overpopulation. He
couldn't admire the sun without thinking of the
people in Africa who saw this blazing majesty in
terms of burned crops and famine. He couldn't ap-
preciate the rain because he knew of the death and
destruction wrought by the monsoon in Asia. The
constant streams of traffic conjured in his sensitive
mind images of the thousands killed and injured on
the roads. Newspaper headlines with their litanies of
catastrophes, murders, and injustices . . . that was

what made up the color of his sky, the temperature of his day, and the quality of the air he breathed.

Since he'd been taking his little red pills, his salvation had come in the form of an absolutely watertight dam between the world and its long-term consequences.

It wasn't that he now didn't care about endangered species, or that he no longer minded about poverty in the world, assassinations, wars, or social inequality (of which he himself was a victim), but he had become more realistic. He was still very upset by poverty and every kind of violence, it really was awful, but . . . well, what could he do about it? He couldn't actually change anything, not by himself. It seemed a sincere sympathy had replaced his painful empathy.

Antoine went for walks, appreciated the simple delights of walking and seeing, experienced the vibrant pleasure in knowing that his heart was beating and he was breathing. He smelled the morning air in the Parc de Montreuil, with his eyes shut tight to the realities of this world. He watched the robins without even thinking of their plummeting life expectancy at the hands of pollution. He enjoyed seeing girls in their pretty summer clothes without wondering whether they had any books in their bags. He took the world for what it was and, without delving beneath the surface, allowed himself to make the most of these free pleasures.

In order to behave like a normal member of society, Antoine asked his neighbors to dinner, or to watch various kinds of matches during which he whooped enthusiastically. He had always had too many doubts, and now he tried to have only partial judgments and to mistrust other people's preferences. While he was still gently settling himself into normality he decided to take the ultimate test to prove how successfully he had integrated himself: McDonald's. Before, it would never have occurred to him to set foot in this lair of imperialist capitalism, this purveyor of fats and sugars, this symbol of the standardization of different ways of life. But he really had changed.

He chose the McDonald's in Montreuil, close to where he lived. In the previous era of his existence (an eternity of a few weeks before), Antoine had always thought that, if he hadn't been opposed to every form of violence, he would have liked to put a bomb in the place. But he had objected to this idea because students and exploited employees worked there, and it wouldn't have been right to injure them and put them out of work.

It was a big, tall, brightly colored building with posters inviting the public to take life lightly, and for a very modest price. A big yellow *M* dominated the façade. A friendly plastic clown with one hand in the air and a perpetual smile welcomed him by the front door. Antoine went in and nodded to the two security guards who were presumably there to protect customers from the powerful gangs of French fry thieves. He reached the counter.

"Hello!" he said to the young woman facing him.

"What would you like?"

Antoine was quite charmed by this relational economy: there was no longer any need to utter a mechanical polite formulaic greeting. He would abstain, then. It was more candid, more honest in fact. He looked at the menu.

"A Best of McDeluxe meal," he deciphered from the illuminated notice, lured by the promise of eating something with the word *deluxe* in its description for just thirty-two francs.

"And to drink?"

"Yes, of course. That's perfect."

"What would you like to drink?" asked the young woman, slightly exasperated.

"A Coke, yes, let's try a Coke."

Of all the mores and customs of this new reality, he instinctively refrained from any form of thank-you. He sat down at a beige table and started to eat his fries as he emptied his 330-ml cup of fizzy brown drink. He peered curiously at one of the fries, dipped it in a mixture of ketchup, mustard, and mayonnaise, and bit into it. Only a few days earlier Antoine wouldn't have been able to make that simple gesture

of eating a French fry without thinking about the
bloodstained history of the potato, the human sacri-
fices that the Aztec civilization made in its name, and
the appalling suffering it visited on the Irish. The
fact that this simple tuber had so many deaths on its
conscience would probably have impeded his complete enjoyment of it. He took a rather awkward
mouthful of his burger; some of the viscous garnish
plopped onto his tray. He had to admit that he liked
it. It was clearly not very good for your health, the
packaging probably wasn't biodegradable, but it was
simple, cheap, very caloric, and it had a satisfyingly
reassuring taste. In fact the taste of it made him feel
as if he had found a family that knew no frontiers, as
if he had joined millions of people biting into an
identical burger at that precise moment. Like an
international choreography, he made the same little
movements in paying for it, sucking up his Coke, and
eating his fries and burger as others danced in tem-
ples exactly like this one all over the world. He had
a subtle feeling of pleasure, of confidence, a new
strength derived from the fact that he was as others,
with others.

Antoine had never taken care of his appearance.
He had sturdy clothes that would take time to wear,
but he had neither the means nor the taste to buy
new clothes; his favorite shop was the secondhand
clothes dealer on the boulevard de Rochechouart. As

for his "hairstyle," it consisted of a simple trim with
the clippers administered by Ganja every two
months.

He asked a hairdresser to cut and style his hair.
In a clothes shop he copied a young man who be-
haved as if he were sure of what he wanted, and
didn't waste time worrying whether the clothes he
was choosing had been made by children. He bought
a pair of Nike sneakers, some Levi's jeans, and an
Adidas sweatshirt. That would be his leisure outfit.
Next he committed a visit to the vast emporium of
the Galeries Lafayette, an offense that would have
been unimaginable such a short time ago. He stepped
into this bourgeois barnyard, perfumed with the
musk of social superiority. On the advice of a salesman whose every word was carefully chosen and
heavily polished he bought a pair of linen pants, a
shirt, and a jacket, all very elegant "but still so, so
coooool, I promise. . . ."

To round off his day he treated himself to a video
game in an arcade where he killed monsters from
outer space. It was very relaxing, and it eliminated
the tensions of a day that he hoped would prove to
be typical of his new way of life. He even enjoyed
exterminating the aliens; once he was locked in com-
bat, he felt responsible, as if the future of mankind
genuinely depended on the agility of his wrist and
the precision of his fingers. He was a hero at last.

Charlotte rang him. She had been inseminated again and she wanted him to take her to a fun fair. They talked about all sorts of things as if nothing mattered, about how the summer had come so late that year, about how the government was so ineffectual, about this wonderful life. At one point she tried to talk to him about the fact that she'd been taken on as part of a team translating the complete works of Christopher Marlowe. After two rounds on the big wheel of this sun-kissed happiness Antoine puked right up in the sky. The two red pills, which hadn't yet been digested, fell into a pool of fries and ketchup. He rinsed out his mouth and took two more pills. He and Charlotte said a vague, casual good-bye to each other.

Standing by a newspaper kiosk and looking at the covers of women's magazines, the light news magazines for men, the advertisements for aftershaves and men's beauty products, and depictions of male sex symbols, Antoine realized that he didn't exactly correspond to the image of the ideal man. An edition of *Elle* magazine had the results of an inquiry about what characteristics in men made women fantasize, and it was with some disappointment that he realized he had none of them. A little while ago, he wouldn't have minded in the least, commenting that these were just the natural counterparts to male fantasies, and that he had deeper, more meaningful qualities. But, under the influence of the red pills, he felt diminished by the fact that he didn't illicit immediate desire. In order to look more like those collective dreams depicted on glossy paper, he enrolled at a huge gym, a brightly lit modern place with exotic plants hanging from the ceiling. He hoped this would help him shape up to the current desirable figure, and gain access to sexual activity.

For an hour a day he lifted weights with his legs, his arms, and his shoulders, using a sequence of repetitive movements. Antoine, exhausted, forgot himself in his exertions; the pain, the sweat, the music of graunching metal and the clunk of weights against the apparatus were turning him into something mechanical, a cog in this great room full of human machines encased within metal machines.

The serious attitude of the other people in the gym convinced Antoine of the importance of his activities. The insistent, hypnotic music set the rhythm for each oar stroke in this muscle-building galley. None of them could look you squarely in the eye, a sense of shame hung in the air, the shame of not having a naturally magnificent body and being forced to make one with this sweat-inducing procedure.

Antoine's body took on the smooth, firm texture of some industrial object; clean lines replaced the more approximative lines of his former figure. Shapes appeared on his tummy, ridges. He was getting stronger, and even though he didn't know how to use this new strength, he was happy to see the steel emerging from his once flaccid flesh. He admired his growing muscles as the stigmata of his normality, visible symbols of his conformity to an ideal of validated beauty. He was strong, he was somebody; he realized now that when he'd been weak and feeble, he'd hardly been anyone at all. Like a construction in Legos, his body fitted together perfectly in his recognition of the world. He now had the same fluid movement as a shark in water, nothing held him back; his physical transformation followed in the footsteps of his psychological transformation. His mind and body no longer hurt, as if— at last—they belonged to that extraordinary species of fish that has no fear of drowning. He didn't even notice that his precious little shy streak had flown from his heart like a butterfly.

Antoine was not unique anymore, he recognized himself in others as if they were living mirrors. And this spared him quite a lot of effort.

Basking in impassive happiness, Antoine felt as if his body were filled with tiny, fluffy goose down, as if this down were circulating in his veins and filling his organs; his heart and brain were overflowing with multi-colored marshmallows. On Tuesday, August 1, he received a letter from the bank informing him that his account was overdrawn. He then experienced his first feelings of anxiety since his treatment had begun. He had been too carefree and had failed to find a source of income while he indulged his newfound lascivious longing for things he would have deemed superfluous a few weeks earlier. He had to find money: life is an animal that feeds off checks and credit cards.

With his command of Aramaic, his degree in biology, and his master's in film on the works of Sam Peckinpah and Frank Capra, along with his countless scraps of diplomas, he had little hope of finding qualified work to match his abilities. The shock of this return to reality neutralized the effects of the Happyzac, and it was therefore in a painful state of awareness that Antoine went to his local employment office. After standing for three hours with other un-

employed people in a room air-conditioned with stress
hormones, a man in a booth called his name (mispro-
nouncing it horribly and without hesitation). Antoine
sat down opposite the man, who was wearing a suit
and twiddling away on his computer keyboard. Five
minutes passed before the man noticed he was there.
He eventually asked him a few questions without
taking his eyes off the computer screen. Antoine re-
vealed his exotic collection of diplomas.

"Forget it," said the man. "You're nuts, right?
What made you decide to study these . . . those
sort of . . ."

"I was interested in them. Oh, and I've nearly
completed a degree course in . . ."

"It's professional suicide. You studied to become
unemployed!"

"Okay, then," said Antoine, getting to his feet,
"good-bye and thank you for your help and support."

"Wait. Don't give up so quickly. Do you have a
driver's license?"

"No."

"You don't? . . . Incredible."

"Actually, according to a study," Antoine
explained sardonically, "the planet's reserves of gas
will be exhausted in the next forty years. There's not
much point in wasting my money for that."

"You mustn't be too picky. You're not exactly
first-choice material. Wait, wait."

The man, who could still look only at his screen, suggested various courses to Antoine, training for jobs that didn't interest him and that would have kept him in poverty. Antoine realized that he was now like a beggar: he had no choice, he would have to take whatever people felt inclined to toss into his hat—coins, subway tickets, meal vouchers, buttons, used gum . . . The man was making quite an effort to find him something (or, it would be more accurate to say, absolutely anything); he was humiliating him with all his professional goodwill. Antoine stood up and left, and the man didn't even notice.

Antoine remembered a school friend named Raphael who'd made a fortune. He rummaged through the box he used as a ramshackle archive, and found his friend's family name and telephone number. Obviously, Raphael no longer lived with his parents, but—whether because they were adorable or completely senile, Antoine wasn't sure—they gave him his number.

Antoine hoped that Raphi (that was his ridiculous nickname) would remember him and the role he'd played in his choice of career during a conversation they'd had in their last year at high school.

Raphi had been very sure of himself and had felt perfectly at ease in any situation; he had that direct, candid way of dealing with people that comes of being sure that you are loved. His aerodynamic mind didn't allow for potentially painful snags on the rough edges of reality; it slid smoothly through the world. Raphi liked Antoine, he found him amusing, principally because he was unaware of the acerbic criticism in Antoine's words; and he was especially curious about this character who didn't gaze on him in admiration. To Raphi, Antoine was exotic, he didn't understand him. From Antoine's point of view, eating opposite Raphi meant he didn't even have to listen to a conversation to know that it wouldn't be interesting. Raphi had the egocentricity of those who speak only in the first person: he talked about himself, and about others in relation to himself, and about what they said about him.

Raphi had been busy chopping a hunk of bread into little pieces, tearing it and twisting it, jumpy behavior that was not normal for him. He leaned over to Antoine's ear and whispered as if they were two American spies in a KGB canteen.

"I have a problem. Can you help me?"

"I would go so far as to launch a massive humanitarian operation," Antoine replied laconically, hardly convinced that these 150 pounds of perfection could really have a significant problem.

"It's very existential, and I know you're good on stuff like that."

"Of course, I have a black belt in ontology."

"Right. I have a choice for my studies. I've been accepted into the best, most sought-after courses. . . . I could follow the path of success and go to one of the really prestigious colleges, then I could join a big company in a major post and end up as CEO, or I could make a career at the top of the civil service. . . ."

"You could become president. . . . ," Antoine said sarcastically.

"Yes, definitely. I could have a brilliant future like that, but I want something else. I want to take risks and do something I'm really passionate about. I don't want to get to the end of my life and realize I've succeeded in everything I've done, I'm rich and loved and all that, but I've never realized my dreams. I haven't spoken to my parents about this, because I don't want to upset them, but I want to throw it all in and follow my heart. I need adventure, to step off the beaten track; I feel as if there's something special and original in me. I have a secret dream, Antoine, a fanatical passion . . ."

"That's great, Raphael," said Antoine, amazed that his classmate was letting himself be carried away by such an apparently irrational passion. "That's great. I have to say you surprise me. I thought you were more down-to-earth, more career-minded."

"It's the poet in me, Antoine, I feel like I have the

soul of an artist. Do you think I should go for it and throw myself into what I believe in?"

"Yes, it's obvious, you should go for it. Shake off your moorings. You'll need courage and patience, you'll have to hang in there to realize your dreams, but, yes, you should live the dream."

Raphi was ecstatic. Overcome with emotion, he took Antoine in his arms, his eyes shining with gratitude. By way of thanking him, he poured him a glass of water.

"Say, Raphael, you didn't tell me what this crazy dream of yours is. . . ."

"I'm going to set up my own brokerage company!"

"Excuse me?"

"Shares, bonds, mutual funds . . . I'm going to do it, Antoine. Thanks to you I'm going to shit gold bricks!"

In the end Raphael's parents didn't take it all that badly; they even gave him a million francs to help his company get off the ground. Ever since, Antoine had had this ridiculous crime on his conscience: he'd created a new capitalist. He had shrugged his shoulders when Raphi had said he would always be there to help him if need be, but right now his bank account was dying of hunger and he could no longer see any moral barriers to undertaking whatever it took to earn some money. When you realize that you're one of the rare few who observe moral principles in their relationships with others, there is a temptation to sink into amorality, not out of conviction or pleasure but simply to avoid further pain, because there is no greater suffering than being an angel in hell, whereas a devil feels at home wherever he goes. Damnation permits everything and forgives everything. Antoine had no choice but to adopt that behavior which consisted of integrating yourself by offering your ideals as a sacrifice. Everything was coming together.

———————

He couldn't talk to Raphael directly: a secretary stonewalled him and asked him to leave his number. An hour later the phone rang in the booth next to the baker's shop. It was Raphi, excited and happy to speak to the friend who'd encouraged him to take his fate into his own hands.

"Antoine! If only you knew how happy I am to be talking to you. You and me, those were good times, weren't they? What are you up to? You have to come over for dinner with your wife, and tell me about your work, that would be fan-tas-tic!"

"I'm single and unemployed."

There was a moment's silence on the other end of the line. It had never occurred to Raphael that his personal success hadn't sown happiness in the hearts of every other human being on earth as well. He was momentarily speechless.

"That's not a problem, you're my guru, Antoine, I can find all that for you. It's the least I can do for you. We have to see each other!"

They agreed to meet in the building at Saint-Germain-des-Prés where Raphi's company was based. Raphi welcomed Antoine into his expansive office decorated with film posters. Their business was soon concluded: Raphi wanted to take Antoine on.

"I don't know anything about the stock exchange. . . ."

"That's just it, you're new to all this, you're not jaded, you won't be influenced by the wrong kind of stuff. That's why I believe in you so damn much!"

"What will I have to do?"

"It's easy: you just have to buy and sell shares around the world. At the right time. To know when a share price is going to go up or down, to listen for things, to trust your instincts. I'm not worried about that at all. I'd bet it all on you."

With great pride, Raphi showed Antoine round his company's luxurious offices, introduced him to his colleagues and to the coffee-making machine.

The atmosphere was hardworking and electrifying but friendly; the working relationships were easygoing, like an egalitarian community. President Clinton had the obedient press corps call him Bill, rather than use his full name, William; it was friendlier, it made him seem like a friend, like someone you're close to (and can forgive easily); but it was especially good at stamping out negative images associated with his position. Using the same emotionally manipulative strategy, Raphael was Raphi to everyone in the company. He had an easy, open, approachable way of dealing with people, and this meant he could exert well-meaning pressure on his collaborators, forcing them—in the nicest possible way—to deliver higher productivity and work longer hours.

Antoine was given a cubicle in the huge room that housed the company's seventy stockbrokers. It was equipped with two microcomputers and a little gray metal desk with lots of drawers and a coffee cup. The market prices in the major stock exchanges around the world unfurled along the walls of the room. For a week Antoine watched what his colleagues were up to; he was given advice; he bought some books to master the financial terms and mechanisms: OPA, NASDAQ, OPE, FED, COB, STOXX, FTSE 100, DAX 30 . . . This new language was so ridiculously simple compared to Aramaic that Antoine cracked it in no time.

His life changed again. His fixed salary, which would easily have been enough for him to live on, was supplanted by a commission on his deals. He gave up his tiny *free* studio for a loft on the rue de la Roquette near the Bastille. As Monsieur Brallaire had still not recovered, Antoine asked Vlad, the wrestler on the seventh floor, to look after him.

He no longer saw Rodolphe, who always tried to bait him with intellectual and polemic subjects, which had lost all appeal for him; without the cement of discussion and dissent, their friendship fell apart. Antoine still took Charlotte up on the big wheel but they no longer talked. Ganja, who was usually so calm, now got angry and announced that they wouldn't see each other until he gave up on his stupid plan to become stupid. Aas dedicated a quatrain to him, saying that they no longer breathed the same air and that, without even crossing a border, they had become foreigners to each other. Antoine parted company with them all one night after a painfully silent evening at their old headquarters, the Gudmundsdottir; he watched his friends disappear into the night, still lit by the glow from Aas's body. It didn't make him feel very sad: he no longer had anything to say to them. Antoine was busy with his new job, his ambition to become ambitious, and his wanting to want designer clothes. He had new friends who had opinions on everything, and he went to concerts and parties with them. He was now living a life that was quite normal to all young people who have the means to live. Antoine was gathering consumer friends, prepackaged, serial friends who wouldn't hesitate not to come and help him if he needed them.

From the outside, you might have thought that he was perfectly integrated in this caste of princes, playing out the role of his Hugo Boss suit without stopping to think about it. But, if you looked a little closer, you would realize he was still keeping his distance—ever so slightly. Still, he never questioned the morality of the people he was with, and never gave an opinion that could be seen as original. Antoine let this new world carry him along and he even took some pleasure in it: the pleasure of freedom within a set framework, of abandoning yourself to the flow . . . which obeyed every curve of the river.

Money, success, integration into a solid, recognized world—all these factors contribute to an economy of the self. There is no longer any need to think about your needs, your mood, your behavior, your friends, or your life, no need to understand or to look any further: the world you're in provides all that right away. Antoine got the keys to a whole life along with the company. It's all down to saving on energy;

it's a lot less tiring (and less tiresome) than trying to
find everything yourself, making it up on your own.
No, that wouldn't be worth the effort, better to be
provided with prefabricated emotions, and preformu-
lated thoughts.

Human beings are really like their cars. Some
have a life with no options, no extras, a life that just
about runs along, can't go very quickly, quite often
stalls and needs repair work. Other lives come with
every possible extra: money, love, beauty, health,
friendship, and success, not to mention airbags, ABS,
leather seats, power steering, 16-valve engine, and
air-conditioning.

———

In mid-August, Antoine was fully adjusted to the
rhythms of his new job; he was a stockbroker like
any other and his work was more than acceptable.
He followed the markets, reacted according to a
combination of instinct and logic, but hadn't
achieved the big deal that would have propelled him
into the inner sanctum of millionaires within the
company. He forgot to think about the consequences
that his speculations and number-juggling might
have on a real world that no longer really existed in
his swaddled mind.

There was only one characteristic that set Antoine apart from his colleagues: he couldn't stand
coffee. He tried to drink a cup of it when he started
out with the company. Result: he didn't get a wink of
sleep for two nights. Since then he'd been drinking
decaffeinated coffee all day long. Now, the cup of
coffee is a question of standing; a good stockbroker
always has a cup of coffee in his hand or on his desk.
Just as a cop has his weapon, a writer his pen, a ten-
nis player his racket, the stockbroker works with his
coffee; it's his work tool, his pneumatic drill, his
Smith & Wesson.

Then suddenly, with no premeditation, Antoine
became rich. He was twiddling away on his two
computers as usual, in his little cubicle amid the hub-
bub of a normal day: rises, falls, cries, phones ringing
constantly, suicides, clicks, shouts, the regular hiss of
the ten coffeepots lined up along the wall . . . He was
tapping away quite happily with a phone wedged
between his ear and his shoulder, selling yens, throw-
ing his hook and line out into the chancy waters of
the market, when—as he reached for his coffee to
moisten his parched lips—he tipped it over the
keyboard of his main computer. There were a few
sparks, a bit of smoke, some crackling, the computer
screen went fuzzy, blinked once, and then everything
settled back to normal in a split second. Except that

his accounts indicated that he had executed a juicy operation to the tune of several hundred million francs. The short circuit had triggered a chain reaction that had culminated in one spectacular financial maneuver.

"I knew it was a good idea taking you on," Raphi told him. "How did you see that one coming?"

"Intuition," Antoine replied, lowering his eyes.

"Yeah, and that can't be learned. But you must have read up on it, you were perfectly in control of the situation, you didn't go to pieces or lose your head. Now, that, my friends, is what I call a smooth operator!"

Everyone in the room clapped, Antoine's colleagues patted him on the back, streamers flew round the room, champagne bottles were opened, and Raphi handed him his commission check. Antoine looked at the sum on the check and, quite unexpectedly, felt moved—as if his own first child had just been born. And so he should have, he'd just had sextuplets: following some inconsequential numeral, there were six perfect zeros lined up on the check.

At that precise moment Antoine didn't remember what he had once known: that you yourself were always the easiest person to corrupt. A red pill spared him from thinking that he might have sold himself and bought himself back at the same time.

In order to grasp the reality of his fortune, Antoine carried off his bonus in small bills. He stepped out of the bank with two suitcases filled with single notes, and piled them up in little bundles on the big olive-wood table in his sitting room. These thousands of rectangles of paper were the atoms of his success. He succumbed slightly to the intoxication of these many small pieces of paper—the embodiment of what was the focus of so much human desire. His head was spinning, and—in spite of himself—he smiled. He was rich; that meant that he'd fulfilled part of his contract by achieving a fantasy shared by millions of people.

But this feeling, which he baptized "happiness," didn't last. What was he going to do with this wealth? If he wanted to be an absolutely normal millionaire, he could never settle for saving the money. Being rich isn't an end in itself; the people in the street had to be the mirrors of his success with their admiration and envy. Antoine realized that by becoming rich he'd completed only half of the journey: he now had to want the things that rich people want. And that struck him as being the really difficult bit. To get rich, all he had to do was spill a cup of coffee over his computer keyboard; but to use his riches, he was really going to have to put his mind to work.

He leafed through magazines and drew up a list of the things he should want. And not want: he was careful not to make the mistakes of the nouveaux riches, an apparently contemptible category of the rich who have only the least important veneer of richness. That being money.

As if he'd become his own Santa Claus, Antoine did his shopping with his sack over his shoulder and his reindeer-drawn sleigh. He bought contemporary art to decorate his loft and cloak his reputation. He went to a prestigious Parisian gallery and chose works by a painter who just had to be a genius given the number of zeros appended to his signature. The gallery owner described him as the new Van Gogh. "In fact," he added, to persuade Antoine, "he even had the mumps." Antoine feigned admiration, gave a charitable little "Oh?" in response to the salesman's venal idiocy, and opened his briefcase. Then he went about buying a luxury car. He didn't know how to drive and had no intention of learning, but that had no bearing on his resolution to conform with this fundamental rite. Nearly everybody buys cars, and for most people the choice is limited by financial restrictions. Antoine didn't have to worry about that, so he found himself confronted with an incredible

choice of makes, models, and engine types. He noticed that different luxury cars often corresponded
with a particular type of wealth: all the younger
millionaires in Raphi's company had sports cars,
and the older thirtysomethings had BMWs or
Mercedeses. Antoine bought a car that would state
clearly that he was young, brilliant, and a millionaire
stockbroker: a red Porsche. The dealer delivered his
car outside his loft, and it stayed there like a neon
sign vaunting his power and success.

In those shops guarded by the Cerberean scorn
the salesmen bear to anyone who doesn't appear to
have the means to make a purchase there, Antoine
was welcomed like a prince once they caught sight of
his golden credit card. He bought beautiful suits that
would give generations to come something to laugh
about but that, for now, propagated his superiority
over the common people who couldn't afford to display such bad taste with such ostentatious composure.

The dictionary definition of *molting* is "a complete or partial change, affecting feathers, hair, skin,
or cuticle, undergone by certain animals at particular
times of year or at specific stages in their develop-
ment." Antoine had molted. He'd given up his
raggedy old clothes for smart new ones; perfumed his
skin with outrageously priced fragrances, exfoliated
it, conditioned it with oils and milks; had massages

and ultraviolet treatment in health spas; and had his
haircut kept in shape once a week in a swanky salon.
Another form of molting comes when a young man
goes through puberty and his voice changes, so it
seemed to Antoine that he had suddenly, in the span
of a few weeks, become an adult. Before the days of
his success, his voice had never seemed very effective
in everyday life, when he needed to ask for something
from a shopkeeper, when he was dealing with someone in some administrative office, or just in conversation; sometimes people didn't even hear him however
clearly he spoke. But now, although he hadn't noticed
his voice changing in any way, Antoine found that
people always heard him, listened to him, and
granted his wishes.

He had molted, sloughed off his former self. In
fact you could even say Antoine had become a sort of
snake. There was little left of the human being he
had once been, as if he had changed species.

His budget had exploded. As well as the major
expenditures, such as the paintings, the car, and the
clothes, he indulged his standing with electrical
equipment, household machines, music centers,
DVDs, and computers. He didn't actually use these
priceless, state-of-the-art machines. Similarly, he
didn't actually eat the great cargoes of fine foods he
stuffed into his outsize American-style refrigerator.
His mind had got as far as the buying stage, but it

hadn't got on to consuming yet. Antoine had kept his simple tastes. His loft looked like a museum of the wonders of modern technology, a cemetery for new machines.

So that his bank account could continue sustaining his practical work as a consumer, Antoine spilled another cup of decaffeinated coffee over his computer keyboard. It hit the jackpot all over again: money is a domesticated animal, a good faithful dog that was beginning to learn the way home to his bank account.

It was the end of the day. All the stockbrokers were clearing up and leaving when Raphi called Antoine into his office. Two young women in sexy evening dresses stood next to Raphi, one on either side of him.

"Antoine!" Raphi exclaimed. "You're incredible, my friend. Here's your bonus."

"Thank you," said Antoine, stowing the millions into the inside pocket of his jacket. "Well, good night . . ."

"What do you mean, 'good night'? We're spending the evening together. To celebrate your stroke of genius. May I introduce Sandy."

"Pleased to meet you," said one of the girls, smiling and holding out her slender hand to him.

"And Séverine," Raphi continued. "She's your date for this evening, you lucky dog!"

Antoine looked at Séverine—her magnificent body,

her enticing appearance, the way she looked at him like she really wanted him—and he told himself there was a problem. Feeling the canines of his personality gently pricking the long-forgotten burial chamber of his conscience, he would have gladly swallowed a couple of Happyzac pills to prevent the danger, but he'd left them at home. He asked Raphi whether he could talk to him alone for a moment. Raphi asked the girls to wait for them by the car. They flounced out of the office with exaggerated sexual challenge.

"I can't believe you've done this to me," Antoine said reproachfully.

"Done what? What are you talking about?"

"You're paying for a prostitute for me. . . . I thought you knew me better than that, Raphael. I'm disappointed. . . ."

"A whore?" Raphi burst out laughing. "You think Séverine's a whore?"

"I thought it was obvious."

"You should have more respect for your own powers of seduction, Antoine. No, Séverine is not a whore."

"Then, why does she want to go out with me?" asked Antoine. "And, more to the point, why does she get that hungry look in her eye when she looks at me? It's like she's looking at Brad Pitt."

"I've told her about you," Raphi replied

smoothly. "That you're a financial wizard, all that stuff. I promise you, you've got what it takes."

"Yeah, right. And who's this Sandy, then? Raphael, you have a stunning wife. . . ."

"Oh, no, you're not going to give me a moral lecture!"

"No, it's not that, but . . . Actually, yes, I will give you a moral lecture because you . . ."

"Are you going to rat on me?" Raphi interrupted him. "Because it's not good to rat. Rats go to hell. You're so uptight, Antoine. Relax."

"This'll make your wife unhappy. You can't do that."

"My wife won't know, so it won't hurt her, so there can't be anything wrong with it," Raphi said simply.

"Why are you doing this?" Antoine asked. "You have someone who loves you. . . ."

"There's more to life than love. There's lust too. Shit, Antoine, this isn't the eighteenth century, we've had the sexual revolution, wake up. People do what they want with their bodies, these girls are liberated."

Raphi reacted with all the haughty conviction of a common-born prince who confuses his privileges for rights and his justifications for the truth. Antoine sat down in the swivel chair facing the desk. He rubbed an eraser over a calendar, staring blankly ahead. He stayed like that for a whole minute while Raphi put some papers away in his briefcase.

Antoine shifted his gaze to Raphi. "On the subject of sexual liberation . . . ," he said slowly.

"What, you want lessons? Séverine will give you lessons . . . if you know what I mean."

"One of your colleagues thinks the same way as you," said Antoine. "Her vote's with you."

"Of course it is, things have changed. You have to lighten up. She's making the most of sex, and she's right to."

"I don't know if you know her," Antoine went on. "Her name's Melanie."

"Melanie?" Raphi asked, paling slightly. "The Melanie from NASDAQ?"

By leaning against the desk, Antoine made his chair swivel round. He was watching Raphi, seeing his reaction, with a little smile on his lips and a touch of sadness just coming to the surface in his eyes. He stood up and took hold of Raphi's shoulder.

"Yep. She's with you on this and, to tell you the truth, she's so liberated she'd sleep with pretty much anyone. Great, isn't it? But the problem is nobody wants to sleep with her. So . . . I thought, seeing as you're so liberated, you could maybe do her a favor. . . ."

"But, Melanie . . . she's really . . . well, you see . . . she just doesn't . . ."

"She's definitely more fun and more intelligent than all your Sandys, but nice too. Is that what you mean?"

"She's ugly, Antoine," Raphi said flatly. "I'm really sorry, but that's the way it is, she looks like a skeleton. She's a cure for Viagra."

"So?"

"So what? What do you want me to say? That's life: not everybody can run the one hundred meters. There are inequalities in nature, I can't do anything about it. She doesn't have the body for it. But there are other sports. She'd do better to put all her effort into love; only feelings can get you by when you're made the way she is. Love is blind. You know the proverb: she's the kind of girl to be friends with, not the kind you screw."

"Is that it?" Antoine asked indignantly. "But . . . Raphael, you don't understand. . . . She wants sex, she wants to have a good time. Just like you, or Sandy."

"I could find out how to find some blind guys. Listen, Antoine, tomorrow I'll offer her an operation to have silicone breast implants, all on the company. That should limit the damage."

"You're really too kind," Antoine retorted sarcastically. "While you're at it, you should just have a dick grafted into her hand. . . ."

"Wake up, Antoine, people don't fantasize about personality. That's not what gives you a hard-on. It may be a shame but that's just the way it is. I can't do anything about it."

"Kirk Douglas said: 'Show me an intelligent woman and I'll show you a sexy woman.'"

"Come on, Antoine, you can't want me to sleep with her just to be consistent?"

"It would have been nice."

Melanie was one of those people who love the things that condemn them, like the poor who admire the rich; just as Raphi didn't want her because she was ugly, she wanted him because he was handsome. A week later she came to work with her blouse unbuttoned to reveal her firm and voluminous new breasts. For some men, this alone was enough to make her visible. She was no longer just a shadow to her colleagues: with her breasts she now fitted into the mold of men's interest.

Raphi was pleased with his magnanimous gesture, but worried about Antoine for what he called his "emotional Robespierrism." With plenty of friendly heckling, he persuaded Antoine to consult a girlfriend of his who ran a dating agency. He assured him that it was a completely trustworthy organization, promised that he wouldn't be committed to anything, and begged him at least to have an interview with his friend. Antoine capitulated just to get Raphi off his back with his libertine catechism and his moralizing. A few weeks earlier he'd still had

some idea of love as a form of art, or at least a craft;
now he lived in a new—and certainly more realistic—world where love was just another form of do-
mestic consumption and segregation.

On the fiftieth floor of an office block that housed
the head offices of high-tech companies, Antoine
went into the teeming premises of the dating agency.
It was open-plan, with employees navigating in
every direction and telephones ringing incessantly;
the clickety-click of computer keyboards distilled
into a music that could have graced the stage at the
National Academy of Music. Antoine was taken to
an office with British decor, cut off from all the activity. He stood there waiting on his own for a while.
The room was brightly lit and very orderly. A few
books on shelves, plants against the walls, unpreten-
tious objets d'art, a sky-blue iMac, a large window.
A woman of about forty bustled into the room, offered him a chair, and walked round behind the
desk. She was wearing an elegant jacket that was
loose enough for her to move freely and perhaps also
to hide what she would have thought of as a few
extra pounds.

"Raphi sent you, didn't he?" she asked, and
didn't wait for an answer before saying, "Right,
let's see what we can find you. Don't be too
picky, you'd be sort of B-list. Do you have any
special preferences?"

131

"Such as?" Antoine asked, perplexed.

"Blonde, brunette, redhead, height, profession. There are quite a lot of criteria. I can't promise to provide you with a spitting image of what you're looking for, but we can get pretty close."

The woman switched on her computer, opened various files, and typed in some words. She seemed exhausted, as if she could hardly go on, but at the same time she was edgy, highly charged. She stared at Antoine, waiting for his list of requirements.

"I don't want to break it down," he said. "Look . . . I think I was wrong to come here. I'm so sorry."

"Does it bother you?" she asked. "But this is how it works, except that instead of using subconscious filters we use scientific ones. You get the same result. We have the best success rate of all the dating agencies, and it's not by chance: we deal with business, not with feelings. The business of feelings, if you like. Where were we? So, no specific profile."

Her fingers smacked the keys violently. The telephone rang but she didn't pick it up. The ringing stopped. She looked at Antoine, noting every detail with her expert eye as if she were evaluating him.

"Somebody of about my own age, though . . . ," he managed.

"Great. Listen, sweetheart, try a bit harder. We make a file on you and what's in it is supposed to make the female clients take an interest in you. So you might as well show yourself in a good light."

"You mean I should talk about the things I care about?"

"Yes, we'll put that at the end," she said a little impatiently. "But first we have to highlight your social position."

"I'd rather not," he said. "I don't want . . ."

"Are you making fun of me deliberately? I don't have time to waste on people who want to be loved for their personalities. Maybe if you were very handsome you wouldn't have trouble finding girls who'd love you for your sense of humor and kindness. But under the circumstances . . . We're not here to moralize, you know, to say it's good or bad, just that's the way the world works, whether you like it or not, that's the way it is, so go ahead and stack all the odds in your favor. Machiavelli said some things about politics that might seem cynical, but that doesn't make them any less truthful. We are the Machiavellis of love. I'm not saying people love for money, hair color, or cup size, but the statistics show that they do have a decisive influence. Your job, muscle tone, height, age, earnings, weight, car, clothes, eye color, nationality, the brand of corn

flakes you eat for breakfast . . . You can't imagine
how many factors influence a decision. Did you
know that blondes have twenty-four percent more
sexual relationships than brunettes? There are truths
in love and sex, and do you know what? Everybody
thinks those truths have nothing to do with them
because they're convinced their little case is different. I've seen the statistics—they're wrong."

"You're generalizing," said Antoine, rallying. "I
think personality does matter, not to the same extent
for everybody but still . . . I know people it matters
to. Maybe you're exaggerating a little."

"Do you think so? It's possible. I am unhappy, so
I have a right to exaggerate and to have a pessimistic
take on all this. All the same, I do think I'm objective, but it could be that in love the truth just looks
like cynicism. To be honest with you it drives me
crazy being so objective, trying to understand that
none of this has any logic to it and that we're not
responsible for any of it. I'd like to stop being objective, to be able to let myself go so that I can hate,
then I would finally be able to really loathe my husband, who left me for a girl of twenty."

She smacked her mouse against the desk, hit one
key on the keyboard, and stood up. She was smiling
but there was a sad kind of nastiness in her smile.
She turned toward the shelves, moved some books
around, and knocked over a little ornament of a

koala bear, which broke on the floor. She knelt down to pick up the pieces.

"I'm so sorry. . . . ," Antoine murmured, going to help her pick up the shards of the ornament.

"Why are you sorry?" the woman asked, frowning. "I won't have you being sorry and criticizing my husband. Who do you think you are?"

"I just wanted to . . . He left you for a younger woman. . . ."

"So what? You're wrong to take my side. I would never have been able to fall in love with a man like you."

"Because I'm not cute enough?"

"No, mainly because you're shorter than me."

"Just because of that?"

"It matters, at least it does for me. Don't ask me why. But I have to admit that it's in the same league as my asshole of a husband who'd rather have a younger woman. There are no innocents in love, just victims."

"It's a bit calculating, choosing by . . . criteria. . . ."

"No, you're wrong there. Nothing's calculated. Everyone is sincere when it comes to love. My husband's really in love with the bitch. He didn't say to himself: 'Oh, my wife's forty, her breasts are drooping, her skin's not as beautiful as it was, she's gaining weight, I'd better replace her.' That's actually the truth, in my opinion, but he didn't say that to himself.

It's just that it happened within those conditions. It's
only afterward that you can rationalize and pick
what someone does to pieces. I could have adored
you, you might have been my best friend, but I hon-
estly wouldn't have fallen in love with you. When I
hear people saying they don't know why they fell in
love with a particular person, it makes me smile.
Maybe they don't want to know, but, as well as the
reasons connected to the meeting of two personalities,
there are the psychological reasons, the social,
genetic . . . Love and seduction are the most subconscious and, at the same time, the most rational forces
we know. Saying there are no reasons means you
don't have to admit that the reasons aren't exactly
glorious, because what good is the truth going to do
anyone? When I asked my husband why he was leaving me for this girl who's young, slim, blond, sexy,
with fabulous breasts and full of life, he said: 'I don't
know, honey, no one knows what makes them fall in
love, it just happens.' And do you know the worst
thing about it? He was being absolutely sincere; the
son of a bitch sincerely believed in that bullshit. The
bastard was sincere. Do you know what the writer
Madame de Staël said? 'In the realms of emotions,
there is no need to lie in order to tell lies.' So, yes, I'm
exaggerating . . . but I'm right to exaggerate
because . . . I'm old, I'm just one of the masses now."

The woman was crying, but she kept on talking, criticizing herself for complaining, cursing her husband and his new fiancée. She didn't even notice when the rather distressed Antoine slipped out of her office.

On a particularly fruitful day of despair Antoine had once told himself that to believe in the truths that force us to bow our heads is to form alliances with the reality they derive from: whoever wants to find proof of his unhappiness will find it, because in human affairs you always find what you're looking for. He had then decided that every truth that made him suffer was a moral, that reality itself was a moral, and one that he could confront with the imagination of his own morals. But even though he was upset as he came out of that office building he didn't remember these ideas. More precisely, he didn't need to remember them: he took two Happyzac pills and the ghost of that disillusioned woman's words disappeared. Antoine rang Raphi, told him what had happened, and said that he should keep an eye on his friend.

A shadow had hovered over his conscience while he had been talking to her, but it had evaporated as soon as he stepped back into the rhythm of life where the days multiply all by themselves.

Those who are perfectly integrated into society

know only one season, a permanent summer, where they tan their happy minds in the rays of a sun that never goes down, even when they're asleep: even in their dreams it's never dark. Antoine had lived in a rainy autumn for twenty-five years; from now on, whether it was winter, spring, or autumn, his mind would know only the uninterrupted reign of summer.

I t was the beginning of

September. The sun was still bright and softly stroking the faces of people on the street through the gentle fingertips of the wind. That evening, Antoine sat in front of his TV channel-surfing, watching interesting and amusing programs. It didn't actually matter much what he watched: the only thing he cared about was the soothing, tranquilizing effect of the TV, its solar glow warming and filling the cave of his consciousness. He sat with the remote control in his hand, zapping. He had covered the remote with thick, silky fabric, and had equipped it with a little motor that made a soft purring sound when he put his hand over it. It was his pet. With his index finger he searched for the programs whose content would act as a pretext, an excuse, for his addiction. Despite four Happyzac capsules, Antoine still wasn't feeling good. This had started a few hours earlier when he had come home from work and found a package outside his door. It was a nondescript little parcel that had been mailed to him, so Antoine hadn't seen any cause for concern as he unwrapped it in his kitchen. He had torn off the paper and sticky tape, and when he'd opened it an explosion had thrown him against the refrigerator. He stood staring at the little opened parcel that contained a paperback edition of Flaubert's letters. His heart gradually settled back into a regular rhythm. He cried; he couldn't stop crying, as if his eyes were trying to wash away the sight of this book on the table, or to put out the fire it had sparked by exploding into his memory. He didn't touch it—he didn't dare. Flaubert's letters had been one of Antoine's favorite books before his transformation. He had loved it and had frequently identified with Flaubert's fumblings, disillusions, and difficulties in the simple act of living and tolerating the age in which he lived. Having this book reappear like this was like biting into a poisoned apple, upsetting his whole organism and reawakening ideas that he thought had been safely locked away. He was pretty sure that this assault was the work of his old friends who were hoping that, by hurting him, they would be able to salvage him. He concentrated his will on fighting against this paper bomb that threatened to upset the steady, unremarkable flow of his life. For fear of contamination, he had left the book on the table and had plugged his mind into the television, his remote purring in his hand.

The colors of the night eased into Antoine's apartment. The moon was sunbathing luxuriantly on the black sand of space. Antoine was trying to hypnotize himself in the cyclopean eye of the TV when a

harpoon suddenly smashed into the screen. Sparks, a
bit of black smoke, the TV host's words distorting,
then nothing, nothing but this harpoon plunged into
the middle of the screen. Antoine turned round
sharply; the remote control fell. There were no lights
on in the apartment, so he could only just make out
the human outline of the harpooner. It wasn't an
extraterrestrial, Antoine thought with some relief. He
realized to his surprise that he wasn't frightened,
probably because of the overdose of Happyzac. He
forced himself to tremble, and he bit his lower lip.
The silhouette indicated a man of average height,
most likely without any bat wings.

The streetlights were going on outside. Now
Antoine could make out the man standing facing
him.

"Danny Brilliant . . . ," he whispered. "You're
Danny Brilliant. Danny Brilliant as a burglar. Are you
going to kill me? Are you some kind of serial killer?"

Antoine vaguely knew this singer who seemed to
have got stuck in the 1950s; he'd quite liked several
of his songs. It was all beginning to make sense:
Danny Brilliant with his Elvis hair, his zoot suits,
and his outdated songs—the guy was a psychopath.
Danny Brilliant laughed. He was dressed in a plain
black suit with a white shirt unbuttoned over his
chest, and black patent leather shoes. The kind of
thing Jerry Lee Lewis would have worn.

"Wrong, wrong, wrong," he said suddenly. "You've got it all wrong, Tony. I'm not Danny Brilliant, or a burglar, and I'm definitely not a serial killer. Would a serial killer dress this nice?"

"I don't . . . know . . . ," Antoine mumbled, "but, you're Danny Brilliant. You talk like him, you've got the same smile, the same hair wax. You're Danny Brilliant."

"That's where you're wrong, Tony: I'm the ghost of Danny."

"Danny Brilliant's dead?"

"No."

"Then, how can you be his ghost?"

"I'm a premature ghost," he explained simply. "It happens. I appear only when the living Danny Brilliant's asleep."

"You're joking."

"Sure am not, Tony. Touch me."

Danny Brilliant, or his ghost, came over to Antoine with an exaggeratedly relaxed saunter, clicking his fingers and with a malicious gleam in his eye.

"I get it," Antoine said, backing away. "You're a pervert."

"I'm a ghost!" Danny said, laughing. "Touch me and you'll see, your hand will pass right through me."

Antoine's hand did indeed go right through Danny Brilliant's premature ghost's body. Antoine found it very funny.

"Hey, that's enough! Hands off! I'm not a game, Tony."

"Could you stop calling me Tony?"

"No problem, Tonio," Danny replied smoothly.

"Okay, you can call me Tony."

"No problem, Tony," Danny said, unruffled, then added: "Do you mind if I have a look in your refrigerator?"

Without waiting for a reply, Danny went into the kitchen. He opened the door to the refrigerator, thereby lighting up the room. Antoine joined him. Danny stood open-mouthed in front of the refrigerator, fell to his knees with his arms spread in adoration and enraptured prayer before this profusion of food. He stood up and filled his arms with Nutella, foie gras, salami, cheeses, blinis, and all manner of victuals. He laid his treasure down on the big kitchen table, sat down on a rather tall chair, and started to demolish the food.

"Ghosts eat, then?" Antoine asked, sitting down on a stool facing him.

"Here'j pfoof," said Danny, with a mouthful of blini spread with foie gras and Nutella. "And you know what else is good? We don't gain weight. We can eat hamburgers all day long, drink as much Coke as we like, we don't gain a single pound. Being a ghost is great, it's a beautiful life, man. Could you pass the Coke?"

"Listen, Danny," Antoine said, "you seem like a really nice guy, you sing nice songs, but I have work tomorrow so couldn't you go haunt someone else?"

"No can do," said Danny after he'd drained half the bottle of Coke and burped quite openly. "I have a mission, that's why I'm here."

"Oh, and your mission is to empty my refrigerator?" Antoine asked.

"No, but that just makes the mission even nicer," he said with his best crooner's smile.

"Couldn't you stop eating for a minute so you could explain without splattering crumbs everywhere? I do the housework."

"Cool it, Tony," Danny soothed. "I've been designated as your guardian angel."

"To warn me of the risks of cholesterol?" Antoine asked. "Who sent you?"

"Can't remember, I was drunk. Anyway, I'm here to get you out of all this shit."

Danny made a sweeping gesture, encompassing the apartment. He burped and picked over the mountain of food. Danny Brilliant's ghost clearly didn't have as much class as the original.

"Well, that's great, then, isn't it?" Antoine said ironically.

"You could say that," Danny agreed as he

attacked a bag of potato chips. "Right, Tony, what kind of life do you have? Are you happy?"

"That's not the word I'd use, but I'm not unhappy, either."

"Neither happy nor unhappy?" said Danny, looking up from a plate. "There's nothing worse. Your life's full of shit."

"Thank you. Thank you for your delicate insight," said Antoine. "To be a guardian angel, don't you go through some kind of psychological training?"

"No, you learn on the job. You're my first, Tony, this is my first time."

"Fantastic, that's really fantastic," Antoine said dryly. He started picking up the debris of food and wrappings. Danny swept the table with his hands, picked up the greasy pieces of paper, the hunks of cake and slices of salmon, and eventually found what he was looking for: the paperback edition of Flaubert's letters. He dusted it down, wiped the grease off the cover, flicked through it, and opened it, turning down the corner of the page.

"There. Do you have a mike, Tony?"

"In the sitting room," Antoine mumbled, feeling more and more tired. "Under the hi-fi."

After sucking up a whole little pot of caviar through a Mickey Mouse straw, Danny went through to the sitting room. He unpacked the mike, put it on

a stand, and plugged it into the hi-fi. A sharp squeal
of feedback blared out.

"Could you pass me my *Best of,* Tony?"

"I don't have your *Best of,* Danny. In fact I don't
have any records."

"That's okay," said Danny, taking a CD out of
his pocket. "I was ready for that. Your stereo has a
karaoke option, that's great."

He put the CD in the player and touched a few
buttons. He held the book of Flaubert's letters open
in his left hand. He tapped the mike, pressed the play
button, and the first notes of his song "Give Me One
Last Chance" oozed round the room without the
lyrics. He moved his head in time to the music, then
started to sing an extract from a letter to Mademoiselle
Leroyer de Chantepie, dated May 18, 1857, following
the rhythm of the song perfectly and adding a few
personal exclamations:

> *People who take life lightly, with their narrow,*
> *   presumptuous, eager minds, want a conclusion*
> *   to everything;*
> *They look for a meaning to life, yeah, and the*
> *   dimensions of infinity, wo-oo-wo!*
> *And with their hands, mmmh, with their helpless*
> *   little hands, they take a fistful of sand,*
> *And they tell the ocean:*
> *"I'll count the grains along your shore," yeah!*

But as the grains run through their fingers,
wo-oo-wo, and the counting takes so long,
They falter and they weep, yeah, they weep.
Do you know what you should do on the
seashore?
You should kneel down upon it or take a walk,
yeah!
Take a walk.
Take a walk, Tony! Yeah, take a walk! Mmmh,
take a walk! Tony!

Antoine was snuggled down on the couch and, in spite of himself, he let himself be lulled by the easy rhythm of the song. The lyrics made his head spin, and he hugged one of the cushions to him. At the end of the song, Danny came to join him. He took him by the shoulders and gave him a gentle, friendly shake.

"Stop driving yourself crazy, Tony. A little is fine but old Gustav was right: take a walk along the beach! You've gotta stop fooling around, you're not a golden boy, that just isn't you. Get rid of the whole lot, that asshole Raphi, get back to your friends and invent your own life. Yeah, invent your life, Tony."

"Everything you say sounds like song lyrics. . . . ," Antoine whispered with a forced smile.

"Professional failing," Danny admitted.

The night was drawing to a close, birds were

singing and flitting among the telephone poles. Danny stood up and dusted down his suit.

"I have to go now; there are other pathetic creatures who need my advice. But I'll keep on watching over you so long as you're still in this mess. You'll get out of it, Tony. Was it Nietzsche who said 'Intelligence is a crazy horse, you have to learn to hold its reins, to feed it the right oats, to groom it and sometimes to use the whip'? Ciao, Tony."

The ghost of Danny Brilliant crossed the room and disappeared in the darkness along the corridor, although Antoine didn't hear the door open. He fell asleep on the couch for a few hours that felt like centuries.

———

In the weeks after the premature ghost of Danny Brilliant's visit, Antoine spoke to no one; he seemed preoccupied. He ignored Raphi and his fellow brokers, and skipped their planned outings to fashionable places. On Friday evening, as he left work, he hailed a cab to take him home. A black van with tinted windows and a picture of a woman riding a dragon airbrushed on its side stopped right in front of him with a screeching of tires. The driver turned to Antoine and pointed a revolver at him. He had an

Albert Einstein mask on his face. The van door slid
open, two other Einsteins took him by the arms and
bundled him into the back. Antoine didn't react at
all; he was so exhausted, so weary, that he didn't have
the strength to fight these creatures set against him.
The Einsteins gagged him, blindfolded him, and tied
his hands and feet. Antoine tried to make a mental
note of the route—where they turned left or right, the
red lights—but after one minute he lost track. After
speeding through the streets, skidding and stalling,
the van eventually stopped. The Einsteins took Antoine out. The warm air of that September evening
felt smooth, as if woven in silk. They went into an
enclosed place, a building, Antoine thought. Someone
grabbed him by the waist and put him over his shoulder. In that position he was carried up several flights
of stairs; he couldn't count them because he was
beginning to feel faint. A door opened. Arms maneu-
vered him into a chair. The kidnappers untied his feet
and tied them to the chair. They left the gag on but
removed the blindfold. For a while he couldn't see
clearly, though he could make out silhouettes around
him, a window. Eventually the images became
clearer, and he could see four people dressed in black
and still wearing the Albert Einstein masks. They
were standing facing him in a semicircle, but they
didn't speak. Antoine tried to speak, but because of

the gag he couldn't articulate at all. He looked at the
room carefully, trying to find some clue, something,
that would explain his kidnapping. Big white sheets
had been stretched across the walls and over the window. A halogen lamp glared behind his abductors,
making them look bigger and more impressive than
they really were; their huge shadows spread over the
whole room and over Antoine himself as he sat bound
to the chair. The wrinkles on the Einstein masks were
exaggerated into terrifying contrasts, and their manes
of white hair gleamed like great hillsides of fire
bleached of their color.

They dragged Antoine in his chair until he had
his back to the window. They put a slide projector
next to him. Then the most extraordinary exorcism
of all time began.

One of the Einsteins took dozens of chicken
heads and feet from a cheap supermarket bag. He
laid them out in a circle around the chair and tied
the head of a cockerel, with its beautiful plumage,
around Antoine's neck. Another Albert Einstein took
a bottle filled with blood and daubed it over Antoine's face. Then all four Albert Einsteins stood
just behind Antoine; the lights went out; the slide
projector started operating.

As the machine projected slides of the great
thinkers of the human race, works of art, inventions
and discoveries, the four Einsteins read—with the

reverent tones of incantation—various passages that
some naïve allopathy deemed would counteract
lethargy. All four of them had a copy of Descartes's
Meditations and Other Metaphysical Writings (in the
striking red cover of the PUF edition), and it was as if
they were holding a book of prayer. They read the
first meditation loudly in chorus, while the images
of artists, scientists, humanists, and *The Simpsons*
succeeded one another on the sheet. They carried on
with passages from Pascal's *Pensées,* from the
Graciãn (and Burgundy wine) enthusiast's *Commen-
taires,* and from the more amusing moments in
Jerome K. Jerome's *Three Men in a Boat.*

The exorcism lasted just over an hour. The clicking of the slide projector finally stopped, and the
abductors stopped their erudite chanting. They
switched on the light and tore down the sheets that
were hiding the room. Antoine recognized his old
studio in Montreuil. The kidnappers took off their
masks, and the sweating faces of Aas, Charlotte,
Ganja, and Rodolphe appeared. They seemed
pleased with the work they had done but it took
quite some gesticulating from Antoine on the chair
for them to think of untying him.

"Have you gone crazy or something?" Antoine
asked as calmly as he could, tearing the cock's head
from around his neck in disgust.

"We just wanted to break the spell on you,

Antoine," Ganja explained. "You'd turned into quite an asshole."

"I have an aunt who's a bit of a voodoo witch," Charlotte volunteered. "She explained how we could free you from the spell you cast on yourself."

"We saved you," Rodolphe declared with his usual self-importance. "You'd become a zombie. We reclaimed you. Mission accomplished."

Aas took Antoine in his arms and hugged him warmly to his huge luminous body. He told him—in octosyllables—how happy he was to see him again. Antoine abandoned any idea of getting angry: his friends had had only the most generous of intentions toward him and, even though it may have been clumsy and could have risked traumatizing him, they'd wanted to save him.

Without mentioning Danny Brilliant's nocturnal visit (which might have given them cause for concern about his mental state), Antoine told them that he'd stopped taking his pills a week ago and had prepared his escape immaculately: he had introduced a virus into the computer system at Raphi's company, which was linked to the global network and would, therefore, cause hugely entertaining financial chaos when the markets reopened the following week.

———

On that night of deliverance they all slept side by side on the white sheets spread out on the floor of Antoine's apartment, like children in a tree house in some magical forest.

Over the next few days Antoine spent his time with his friends, having fun and rediscovering the pleasure of their interdependence.

One morning the police came, knocked at the door, and arrested him. Raphi had fled to Switzerland with some of his savings. Deeming his exile to that humorless land to be punishment enough, the law did not insist on his extradition. The case came to trial very soon, and Antoine had to pay a fine that drained all the money he had earned; all his worthless assets, his paintings, and his car were seized; and, as no one had been injured, he was given only a six-month suspended sentence. Antoine felt it was a fair price to pay for Raphi's exile and for managing to make a few million francs disappear.

It was one of those mornings on the brink of autumn when the moon manages to survive into daytime. The sun was nowhere to be seen in the sky, but its delicate presence could be felt on every natural and urban thing as it emanated from flower petals, from the venerable Parisian buildings, and from the tired faces of passersby. It is in the fruitful sacrifice of the passage of time that easily traumatized eyes perceive the only true kinds of Eden, those in which architecture can be felt.

On that Sunday morning, Antoine woke at eight o'clock. In the mingled waters that lie between sleep and wakefulness he thought he heard singing.

He climbed out of bed, stretching. After putting some water on to boil he took a shower. Once the tea had infused he stayed there for a moment in front of the window, watching the steaming green liquid. There was a robin on a branch outside, apparently striking a pose to trigger Antoine's memory; the last of the summer sun exhaled a permanent flashlight into the atmosphere. Antoine didn't drink a drop of his tea; he put his cup down by the window and walked out of his studio.

He walked all the way to the Parc de Montreuil, slipping sinuously among cars and people moving past. He was in a hurry, with his laces untied and his hair still damp and unbrushed. At this time of day the park was as good as empty: a few old people out for walks, women getting their children into the fresh air, and a woman in a big hat who'd set up an easel on the grass.

Antoine walked aimlessly as if he felt lost in this calm, unruffled place. He sat down on a bench next to an old man leaning on his silver-handled walking stick. The old man was wearing a gray felt hat with a black silk ribbon round it; he turned his head toward Antoine slightly, then resumed his position as a weary sentry. Antoine looked over in the same direction and at first he saw nothing, but then—by screwing up his eyes and looking very carefully—he saw a young woman right in front of him. She examined Antoine intently, put her head on one side, and crouched down to look at him more closely, as if he were a sculpture, then she held out her hand to him. Antoine responded with automatic courtesy and shook her hand. He wanted to talk, but the young woman put a finger to her lips and motioned to him to get up and follow her. They moved away from the bench and the old man.

"I'm looking for some friends," said the girl, glancing at Antoine and then at their surroundings.

"What do they look like?"

"Like you, maybe. You looked like someone interesting sitting there on that bench, so I told myself you'd want to be one of my friends. You seem pretty good quality. Superior quality."

"Superior quality?" Antoine asked, perplexed. "It sounds like you're talking about ham."

"No, not ham. I don't eat meat."

"Do you eat your friends?"

"I don't have any friends anymore," she said simply. When Antoine said nothing, she added, "You'll have to stay with me on this. Seeing as I've said something pretty strange there, you're supposed to ask me why."

"My agent forgot to send me the next bit of the script so . . . why?"

"Why what?" she asked with a very convincing portrayal of astonishment.

"Why don't you have any friends anymore?"

"They rotted," she said casually. "I hadn't noticed they had an expiration date. You have to watch out for that. My friends started to have traces of mold on them, green patches, it was pretty gross. What they said was really beginning to smell bad. . . ."

"That could be dangerous," said Antoine.

"Yes, they could have given me salmonella."

"Did you put them in the trash can?"

"No," she said, "didn't have to, they threw themselves away with their pathetic lives."

"You're very harsh."

"I'm sorry, but that's not your line," she said sweetly. "You're supposed to say: 'You're incredible.'"

"There have been some last-minute rewrites."

"I'm always the last to know!"

The girl stopped abruptly and smacked one of her hands to her forehead. She turned to face Antoine, looking slightly stunned with her eyes wide open.

"We forgot the introduction scene! We forgot the introduction scene! We'll have to go right back to the beginning. Come on, let's go back to the bench."

"You know," Antoine said, stopping her, "we could do a link shot. That's what the editing's for."

"You're right. Let's walk a little way without saying anything and then we'll introduce ourselves. Action!"

They walked along the little paths in the park and on the grass, gazing at the trees and the birds. It was warm and the air had a bright, almost iridescent color. Never had the month of September been more lovely; it was ingenuously unaware of the encroaching autumn, standing proud and burning with the last of the summer's strength as if it would go on forever.

"Hey," the girl said spontaneously, "my name's Clémence."

"Pleased to meet you," Antoine replied cheerfully. "I'm Antoine."

"I'm so pleased to meet you," she said, shaking his hand, then after a few seconds' silence she went on: "Now, Antoine, let's go back to the bit where you were saying I'm incredible."

"I actually said you were harsh."

"That's very unfair of you. Don't you ever judge anyone?"

"I try," said Antoine, "but it's difficult."

"My theory is that you can understand and judge. We only judge in self-defense because, well, who tries to understand? And who understands those who try to understand?"

"Lacenaire said that only the condemned are entitled to judge."

"Well, that's fine, then," said Clémence with a shrug. "We're condemned. I've always been condemned; ever since I was a little girl I've been judged and given silent sentences. Don't you think what I'm saying is really beautiful?"

"Like what?" asked Antoine.

"Like: everything. The whole of society is a sentence passed against me. Work, studies, modern music, money, politics, sports, TV, models, newspapers,

159

cars. Now, that's a good example: cars. I can't cycle or walk wherever I like and make the most of this city: my freedom is completely condemned by cars. And they smell, they're dangerous . . ."

"I'm with you on that," said Antoine. "Cars are a disaster."

They bought some cotton candy. Nibbling at it and tearing off pink swathes, they soon finished it, leaving their lips and fingers sticky with sugar.

"And another thing," said Clémence. "If you ask me, the big divide in this world (well, apart from the whole social-class thing), the big divide in this world is between the people who used to go to parties and the people who didn't. And this split in the human race, which goes back to junior-high days, goes right through life in different guises."

"I wasn't invited to parties," said Antoine.

"Neither was I. They were scared because I said what I thought, and I thought some pretty bad things about my classmates. I hated nearly everybody. It was great. But now, now that they've realized how incredible we are, they want to ask us to their grown-up parties and pretend nothing happened, like everything had been forgotten. But no, we won't go."

"Or if we did, it would only be to steal a few of the hors d'oeuvres and some bottles of Orangina."

"And to hit them all over the head with a base-ball bat," said Clémence, miming the action.

"And then we'd finish them off with golf clubs, it would be more elegant."

"Such class, such grace!" Clémence cooed.

Still talking, they left the park, walking side by side. Clémence skipped, picked flowers, and chased the birds, clapping her hands to scatter them. She was about the same age as Antoine, and her personality kept turning somersaults, very serious one moment and then, seconds later, completely relaxed and lighthearted.

"Why shouldn't we be allowed to criticize?" she suddenly exclaimed candidly, spreading her arms wide. "Or to think people are idiotic and weak, just because it might make us look bitter or jealous? Everyone behaves as if we were all equal, as if we were all rich, educated, powerful, young, white, beautiful, male, happy, healthy, driving big cars . . . but that's not true. So I have a right to complain, to be angry, and not to smile beatifically the whole time, but to say what I think when I see things that are not right or fair, and even to insult people. I have every right to complain."

"Okay," said Antoine, "but . . . it can get exhausting. Don't you think there could be better things to do?"

"You're right," Clémence conceded. "It's ridiculous wasting energy on stuff that isn't worth it. It's much better to save your strength for having fun."

"And taking a walk on the beach."

"Taking a walk on the beach . . . That's from a song, isn't it?" Clémence asked, vaguely humming a tune. They were walking along the sidewalk among the crowds of working people and the jobless, students, the very old and the very young. The shops, bakeries, and banks never emptied of the brightly colored corpuscles that each person represented within the city's vast and complex circulatory system. A car sped past them, hooting, and then stopped at a red light ten meters farther on. Clémence took Antoine's arm.

"Close your eyes," she told him. "I have a surprise for you."

Antoine closed his eyes. A soft, warm gust of wind ruffled their hair as Clémence guided Antoine, pulling him by the arm. She took him to the middle of the road; there was a black car coming toward them, about one hundred meters away.

"Okay, you can open your eyes now."

"Clémence, there's a car coming," Antoine announced calmly.

"You promised me you'd trust me."

"No, I did not, I never said that."

"Oh," said Clémence, "I forgot to ask you that. Trust me, okay?"

"Clémence, the car . . ."

"Swear that you trust me and stop shaking, you

wimp. You have to stay still, it's very important. Swear it!" she insisted.

"Okay, I swear. I won't move, I won't . . . move. . . ."

The car was only thirty meters away, the horn was screaming to get the two of them off the road. Antoine and Clémence still didn't move; people were watching them. At the very last moment, Clémence tugged Antoine's arm and they fell onto the sidewalk. The black car hurtled past, growling angrily and baring its teeth.

"I saved your life," said Clémence, standing up and helping Antoine to his feet. "I'm your heroine. That means we're connected for life. We're responsible for each other from now on. Like the Chinese."

"I think I've had enough excitement for one day," said Antoine.

"Do you have a set amount you can't exceed?"

"Yup, that's right, otherwise I overdose. Don't tell me overdoses of excitement are fantastic, I'm not used to them."

Famished from all the excitement, Clémence and Antoine agreed to go and have lunch at the Gudmundsdottir with Aas, Rodolphe, Ganja, and Charlotte and her girlfriend. But, because it was still a few hours until lunchtime, they decided to play ghosts. Clémence explained how the game worked to

Antoine: they had to behave like ghosts, looking at
people on café terraces from every angle, walking
through the noisy streets and shops making spooky
noises, taking advantage of the fact that they were
invisible, wandering aimlessly, acting as if they had
disappeared in the eyes of the world. Rattling their
chains and raising their arms in terrifying gestures,
Clémence and Antoine set off to haunt the city.